The Fantastic

Adventures of Being Lost

in Space:

Past the Sun's Light

By E.W. Wooten

Contents

Prologue

Life on Earth, the life we all know, is already unbelievable in its existence. On a chunk of rock, flying through space and circling a flaming orb of Hydrogen gas, there are millions of forms of life, including plants, animals, and many things inbetween. Most unbelievably, out of all of these creatures, there is you, a person, reading this story or maybe even listening to the oration of it. You are an extraordinary individual that can change the world by putting your mind to it. Quite incredible, really. However, this story is about someone who is, distinctly, not like you. Not to say he is not incredible, but he has no idea what it is like to be happy.

On an Earth, much like your own (maybe it even is), lived a boy many years from now, if time even matters when discussing another Earth, that is.[1] This boy, Jason Calloway, was completely average in almost all regards, even below in a few, or so he thought. He was average in height for his age, which is only 13 at the start of this story, and the lad had the most common brown hair with the dullest brown eyes. You would have called him pale, if he was not almost always sunburned from living outside.

Oh, yes, this boy lived alone and homeless. Despite believing himself to be merely average, he lived a life of despair. It started when he was born. Because, even with the advances your kind made in medicine, the poor child's mother did not make it through Jason's birth. Left alone with his father, who was absolutely unlucky in his own right, Jason lived a peaceful, average life. Until he was 8, anyway. It was on Jason's 8th birthday that his father had disappeared. Joshua left early, from his home, on that day, needing to pick something up, and due to the family having a serious lack of luck, never returned.

It was on that day, the day his father abandoned him, that Jason started to become very unlike you. He lost his sense of wonder and his desire for the fantastic. Jason's love of adventure was snuffed out almost entirely with without hope to ever rekindle it. Unfortunately, his life got worse from there. By the time he was

12, the child could hardly stand being alive anymore, and he had no concept of being able to do anything to change that feeling. This once happy, hyper imaginative, intelligent boy had the traits that made him special stolen away from him by life. It certainly did not help that his foster family put him to work in a salt mine at age 11.

You see, his foster family were absolutely evil. The only value they found in life was their own. So if they were to take in some poor orphan, they would put him to work. From when they took him in at age 8 until he turned 11, he spent most of his time doing almost nothing besides chores for his would-be adopters. It was then at 11, right after he passed his basic educational courses, that his foster family pulled him out of learning to work in the Salina Salt Mines. Salt, despite being far too common on Earth, turned out to be in high demand when humans started to get into galactic trade.

Do not be surprised at that information. Of course, aliens are real. Even on your Earth, it is only a matter of when you will discover them, as opposed to if. We will get around to meeting many of these galactic neighbors, later of course, as an extraordinary individual such as yourself would hate to have the interesting parts of the story expositioned away at the start. Just know, Earthlings, in that time, were now starting to explore space and form bonds with many forces beyond the solar system, and many of them treated sodium chloride as if it was a drug beyond any other. This was due to two reasons. First, most aliens had never thought of adding any kind of spice to their foods, and second, because several species figured out how to generate almost infinite energy from forcing the atoms of the molecules to unbind and rebond.

It was on the way back from the salt mine, one day, that Jason witnessed his foster family being rightfully arrested for embezzlement and child abuse. However, instead of reentering the foster system or even being brought to testify to the crimes of the false family that had unfortunately taken him in, Jason took his pay from the salt mine that week and bought a bus ticket away from his small town home to the largest space port city in the world, Neolandia.[2] It is here, a half year later, that our exposition ends and we find our average would-be protagonist strolling down an empty street after having successfully stolen some old bread from a bakery's dumpster.

Chapter 1: In An Alley

Jason walked down this empty street quite often. Most of the buildings were abandoned due to the high price of rent in Neolandia. It really was a city that you visited, not lived in. Old shops, that at one time must have been the cornerstone of some romantic neighborhood, stood abandoned. Jason wondered if parents brought their children here to buy new clothes or if those same kids dragged the adults across the street to what must have been an antique toy and collectible store. There was still a sign with some fantasy knight fending off a dragon decaying in the window.

Jason sighed as that sign crossed his mind. It reminded him of his father. Even on the day he left his son, he was telling the young boy stories of knights and magic. Jason used to dream of being in a story like that. Now, he barely dreamed of finding fresh pastries in a dumpster.

The young teen, usually, only left his alley that he had made his home because he did not know what else to do. Besides trying to survive, that is. Fortunately, the kid did leave the alley that day.

On his walk past these failed shops, Jason noticed something odd. Another person was on this street. No one visited that part of town anymore. Moreover, this other person was sitting by a building, back to the wall and hugging his knees that were brought up to his chest. Jason considered crossing the street so he did not have to pass by, but, as he got closer, he noticed that the other individual was another kid, maybe a year or two older than himself. He was in a terrible state, too. The kid's clothes were torn like he had been in a fight. The stranger's dirty blonde hair was tangled. He looked as if he had sat out in the rain from the last two nights and did not have a place to get dry.[3]

Jason thought to himself, *Well, I would like, if I was that kid, for someone to at least ask me if I was okay. I wish anyone would ask me if I was okay.*

As if reading his mind, though it was really just empathy, the tattered clothed boy raised his head and looked at Jason.

"Hey, kid, you alright? You look like you're in the dumps," This stranger asked as he rose to his feet to greet our pessimistic protagonist and to reveal he stood only a couple inches taller.

Taken aback by the question, Jason replied, "Yeah… yeah, I'm fine. Speaking of dumps though, it looks like you couldn't even find one of those to stay in."

The strange teen scratched the back of his head and smiled, "You are probably right. I got into a fight today at the space port. Apparently, you aren't allowed to stow away on any ship you want. I'm also kinda hungry. I've barely eaten since I got here a week ago."

"You might be in luck then. If you aren't picky, I got some bread I found in a dumpster."

Jason pulled out the last loaf of bread he found and held it out for the stranger. The stranger smiled even wider and snatched the bread out of the kid's hand and started shoving bites into his mouth. Jason could barely make out the teen's thanks through his stuffed mouth.

"Hey, I know a homeless guy when I see one. If you don't have a place to stay, I've got an alley I've made home. It is down a block, by a big warehouse of sorts," Jason offered since he felt bad over the other boy's circumstance.

The stranger smiled after swallowing the last bite of bread.

"Race you there then!"

The older teen took off at a half sprint. Jason was dumbfounded, but he also did not want to lose a race to a starving stranger. So, Jason took off in a full sprint after. It was a good race.

The stranger would have easily won except he ran past the alley and had to be called back.

The two boys laughed as they entered the dry alley and began talking about the reasons why they ended up homeless in that city.

"So, kid, let me get this straight, you came to Neolandia not in hope of finding an adventure or a new life in space, but because you figured you had better odds at living without a home here," questioned the adventurous Timolas Thomas Tymes, the strange homeless youth.

"That is correct, I figure a box in an alley is better than the salt mine back home," replied the rather cynical Jason Calloway.

"That is ridiculous, the homeless come to this city to sneak onto space ships, to leave Earth. That is why any of us are here!"

"I just figured that if I had to resort to begging, more people would be here in the city, with higher paying jobs, and I would have better odds at getting UC transfers and have more opportunities to scavenge food. You know, have better chances to not starve."[4]

"Well, that will make it easier to survive. At least, until I can hop on a spacecraft to head off on my adventure."

"You are welcome to stay here in my alleyway until then… What was your name again?"

"Timolas Thomas Tymes, call me 3T," this dirty blond, green eyed teen stated.

"Jason Calloway, call me Jay."

"So, Jay, what makes this alley so special?" 3T asked, confused over why Jason would choose such a remote place to stay.

"Hmm, the alley happens to be one of only a few with a covering between buildings in this neighborhood, so it is easier to stay dry."

"That's a plus," 3T said, sarcastically.

"Well, we also happen to be next to some kind of warehouse, which has armed guards that come in and out. So, no one starts any trouble for fear of them."

"Why do they let you stay here?"

"We are just kids, probably, and this side of the building has no entrances or even windows, so what is the harm, right?"

"Yeah, shelter and safety… but what do you do for food?"

"That is the best part," exclaimed Jay as he pulled two loaves of bread from his dirty, brown jacket. "There is a bakery, right down the street, maybe two blocks over, and the lady who owns it throws out the old goods every day around 1700. She never sells anything. So, there are always plenty of scraps."

3T was confused for a moment before he asked, "So, Jay, why is it 1700 and not 5PM? Are you a military kid or something? I've never heard someone use that system."

"No, you really are new here. Apparently, the people in the city, and in space travel in general, thought it was more classy when talking to aliens. Less confusing. It is something I picked up recently, actually. The clocks all use the 24 hour system here, if you haven't noticed."

"The city is weird."

"Yeah, it is."

The two boys sat quietly, eating their remaining old bread, not knowing that their friendship would lead to many possibilities opening up to them.

They spent the next few weeks together. When 3T was not scheming on how to smuggle himself onto a spaceship, that is. He preferred to try civilian galactic cruisers, but security at the civilian port always seemed to be a step ahead of the teen. It was when he tried the old Victorian era lady disguise trick, finding the outfit in a 'discarded' travelbag, that he ended up on a list of people banned from the port.

The civilian space port always seemed to be busy. Humans had made ships that could travel to Mars in less than a day and could reach the edge of the solar system in only a week. Those were the ones that could be produced for inner-solar travel. A few ships at the port had been designed by humans to get to neighboring star systems in a few weeks. It was uncommon, but since this civilian port was the largest on Earth, a few alien ships landed at the port. The security on them was far greater, and even 3T knew that he would have no hope in sneaking on one of those. However, these ships brought in just enough aliens to keep any trip to the port exciting. Whether it was the tree-men from Olnar II seeking a good vacation in the jungles of Earth or the Ultorians, who were like both lion people and lizards that had three sets of eyes, site-seeing this planet on the edge of their empire.

That was a short trip, thought Tim, after noticing the ship he had finally sneaked onto was landing after only a couple of hours.

The ship was a smaller vessel and 3T overheard the boardees state it was heading to Mars. Tim did not much care that it was only going a planet over. He loved the idea of Mars, the red planet turned green. It was Earth's greatest triumph of the previous century. They made life for humans and many other things sustainable and even thrive on a foriegn world where it previously was not. Unfortunately, the cargo door slid open and 3T stared out in horror, as he saw a site that clearly was not the planet Mars.

"This isn't Mars!" Exclaimed Tim.

"No, this is New Mars," said the exasperated bagboy, who seemed not to care about a stow-away.

"Yeah, I know, the Ocean gave it away," replied Tim.

Tim Tom was staring off into the distance, quickly realizing he was on the floating city of New Mars, oddly constructed where Florida used to be.[5]

"I've got to get back to Neolandia. I can't leave Jay behind for… for this," fussed 3T as he gestured incredulously at the city and the Atlantic Ocean.

"Just stay in there then," said the bagboy as he unloaded another bag. "I don't get paid to report stow-aways, and this ship will be returning to the Neolandia port this evening."

"Yeah, thank you. At least it is only a couple hours. I didn't even know that Earth to Earth transport went through the space port."

"Most of the small ones don't, but some people just don't trust teleport travel. Too many stories of missing fingers. Now shut up and duck back down before we both get in trouble."

It took several hours for 3T to return home, all in which time Jason had a productive day dumpster diving. While 3T stole some very expensive sugar waters from the bags in the cargo hold, Jay discovered several new pastries in the bakery dumpster and found some decent material to use as blankets in the dumpster near the tailors another couple of blocks over. It was early evening when 3T came slugging his way back into the alley, exhausted from being tossed from the spaceport after being discovered in the cargo hold after the ship returned to Neolandia.

"So, 3T, you make it into space today?" Asked the smug Jason.

3T, looking up from his knees, smiled and said, "Yes, Jay, I got all the way to Mars but decided to come back because I didn't want to miss dinner with you."

"Good deal, since Miss Jerry at the bakery threw out these today," stated Jason as he pulled two large potato pies out of his makeshift satchel.

Shocked, 3T said, "You might be the best friend ever, Miss Jerry needs to start making these every day!"

"Thanks, though I think she just follows *Mama Mack's* recipes.[6] Hey, did you snatch anything today? You going to pull your own weight for a change?"

3T smiled wider, "Duh, how about a couple of bottles of De Salina brand solar water?"

"No freaking way, that stuff is like 20 UC a bottle!"

The two friends, who both desired different things in life, sat and joked about their day as they ate a potato based pastry taken from a dumpster and drinked a stolen, fancy water. It was strange for Jason. He had not smiled and laughed like that in years. It was strange for 3T, as well. He had a dream of leaving Earth; he knew his fortune was waiting for him in the stars. A fortune that he needed.

3T had asked Jay the same question several times since they first met, but the answer always was the same.

"Listen, Jay, why not come with me? Take to the stars with me."

"Look, 3T, I don't want adventure. I don't want to travel the stars. I want to live the dullest of lives. Besides, I'm cursed.

The ship would probably die in space or we'd crash into a toxic world if...wait... Did you see that guy pass by?"

Sure enough, a shadow caused by the street lights of the early evening did pass by while Jason was explaining himself. No one, hardly, came down that road that time of night.

"Um, yeah, that guy was hanging out near the alley with some small, cloaked fella this morning when I left and was still there when I got back a bit ago."

"Old guy, right? Stumbly beard, grey hair?"

"Yeah, a little hunched, too."

"I think that guy has been hanging out around here for a few days. Sometimes with that smaller person."

"I wonder what they are..." 3T paused as two shadows engulfed the alleyway, the home that the two boys shared.

In the mouth of the alley, stood two figures. The first, a larger figure, stood in a hunched position. He had on a dark maroon jacket and jeans that were clearly designed for both comfort and utility. His hair was a washed out grey, and his eyes glowed just a tad in the shadow of the alley. The second figure, clad in all black and dark grey, hid their features under a cloak and hood. It was this second, more mysterious, figure that spoke first with a serious, feminine voice.

"Boys, I am sorry to inform you that I plan on destroying your makeshift home. It cannot be helped. I have discussed, with my associate here, when we discovered that you had made a home in this alley, about our options. We have determined there is only one solution, one possibility, that will make the inevitable destruction of this unfortunate abode fair to all parties. The two of you are hereby invited to steal the spacecraft hidden within this warehouse with me and then travel into the abyss of space to go on the greatest adventure a human has ever known."

Chapter 2: Goodbyes Aren't Forever

"I'm in/No way!" Yelled 3T and Jay, respectively.

"That's wonderful, just what I… wait, you don't want to explore space?" Asked the mysterious lady.

"Of course I want to explore space! That is the whole point of being here!" Exclaimed Timolas.

"I think she was talking to me. I have no desire to do anything. I would only bring trouble, and I personally would prefer you not to destroy this alley. It has the best cover from the sun and rain," fussed Jason.

The stranger threw back the hood of her cloak, revealing the visage of a teenage girl with jet black, short hair and eyes that looked very similar to Jay's own brown ones.

"That is absolutely the dumbest thing I have ever heard. Not wanting to explore space, ridiculous," Complained the stranger.

"You have your dreams, and I have mine. It's just that mine is doing nothing and accomplishing nothing. Besides, who in space are you, anyway?"

"Yeah, that is kinda important to know before we steal a ship together," Added 3T, crossing his arms thoughtfully, siding with Jay despite finding the stranger very attractive.

"My name is Captain Amelia Hush, soon to be owner of the greatest space exploration craft made by man. This, here beside me, is my pilot, Mister Larriott."

The older man stepped forward and exclaimed with a raspy voice, "Pleasure, boys."

Up close, Larriott was creepy. He seemed human at first, but the more you looked, the more you would question if he was some form of robot or alien. His eyes had only irises and no pupils. His mouth had some kind of metal behind the teeth. Finally, his nose was shaped like a sea sponge.

"You look younger than me, and you are a captain?" Asked 3T, looking nervously away from Larriott.

"Well, I did just turn 15, and the ship I am captain of is not quite in my possession, yet."

"Yeah, you said it was in this warehouse?" Stated Jason, questioningly.

"Yes, we have discovered that Antonio De Salina, the world's richest man, as you know, has hidden a secret escape ship here in case the world is doomed at some point. Personally, I find a ship that isn't being used for its intended purpose, traveling the stars, to be a waste of resources. So, being a generous woman…"

"You are younger than me, calling yourself a woman," 3T mumbled to himself.

"Do you want to get a ride on my ship? I will leave you here with your friend!" Exclaimed Amelia, finally dropping her polite guise and revealing a stern demeanor.

"Sorry," squeaked 3T.

"Sorry?" Repeated Amelia, crossing her arms, expecting something more.

"Sorry, Captain."

"Forgiven, Mister… Oh, what are your names, by the way?"

"Timolas Thomas Tymes, call me 3T."

"Jason Calloway, call me Jay. Though, we won't be talking much."

"Well, Mister Calloway, I am truly sorry to be destroying your alley, as the building is going to collapse when we take off. Also, since we will be using a hidden door in this alley, even if the alley survives, the guards will probably detain you. Since, you will be an accessory to our crime, afterall. So, it would be best for you to get away from here."

"I've lived in this alley for months. There are no doors in this alley," Jason argued back.

Without saying a word, Amelia walked to the middle of the alley, reached towards the wall, felt it for a few seconds, and then pushed a small, pin sized button. She stepped back and smirked at the boys. A slight yellow glow appeared, as if surrounding a doorway. Slowly, the wall inside the glow started to slide down and disappear. An opening showed the inside of the building, and a long hallway leading both to the left and the right.

"I guess these people aren't crazy, 3T. So, you're leaving, huh?"

"Yeah, I guess if there is a hidden door, there is probably a spaceship, too."

"I'm going to miss you, 3T," Jay said as he realized the only friend he ever had was about to leave him.

"Yeah, I'm going to miss you, too. Hey, I will be back someday though! So, this isn't goodbye for good, you know, and you could, also, still come with us! Larry and Captain Amy seem like great people. Not counting them stealing a spaceship and blowing up a building."

"I'm pretty sure his name is Larriott, not Larry. You know I don't want to go to space, 3T, or go on some adventure or anything like that. That life isn't for me. I will wait for you to come back, though."

"Fine, but you look after yourself," 3T said, tears starting to form in his eyes.

"That is Captain Amelia Hush. I do not like nicknames, Mister Tymes," interjected Amelia. "Now come along. We do not have much time. Hug your friend goodbye and follow us in and quickly, at that."

3T did move forward and gave Jason a hug. That was the first time he had been embraced, shown love in any form, since his father left over 5 years prior. Jason, with tears streaming down his face like rivers, hugged his friend back. Jason would truly miss Timolas. They lived like brothers for the last month. However, Jay knew it was only a matter of time before anyone he cared about left him. It was the real reason he refused to go to space. It was better to be abandoned on Earth than in the void of space, thought the naive boy.

The two boys separated. They, without making a sound, simultaneously, smiled goodbye and turned away from each other. 3T turned towards Amelia and Larriott, who he noticed had a small travel bag in one hand. They gestured him on. The three of them moved through the newly formed door and left towards their future. Jason had turned towards the exit of the alley and, immediately, started to leave. It was right before he stepped out of the alley that he looked back over his shoulder to see his friend disappear inside the building.

Jay turned his head back away and let it drop. He stood there a minute before a horrible sound shook him out of his depressive stupor. Voices were coming from the main street in front of him. The words he heard changed the course of this poor, average kid's life.

"I didn't even know there was a side door, Mick."

"Yeah, Frank, me neither, but the boss just called and said a silent alarm was activated from the door."

"Fine by me. I just hope there is something to shoot. I hate carrying this thing and never getting to use it."

"Neutralize any and all suspicious individuals were the orders. So, we can only hope."

Jason barely glanced out of the alley in the direction of the voices. Two guards, both carrying N-Class laser rifles, were coming out of the front of the building and heading in the direction of the alley.[7] Jay did not have time to think of what to do. He took off in a full sprint back towards the alley door, terrified for his friend and the odd strangers who were all very suspicious individuals. Jason ran through the door, and then he turned the same direction as his friend had traveled. It was only a few seconds before he crashed into the group, who had become stuck at a literal crossroads. The three youngsters went crashing to the ground, Larriott stepped out of the way having seen many kids come running at too fast of a pace in his lifetime.

"W-what do you think you are doing?!?" Cried Amelia as they started to get up off the floor.

"Jay! You changed your mind!" Cried 3T at the same time as Amelia.

"The alarm went off, guards are coming!" Cried Jason, quieter and out of breath, but still at the same time as the others.

"Guards!?" Both 3T and Amelia exclaimed.

"Yes, and with some terrible looking weapons."

"We've got to run, then! Captain A, which way is it," 3T suggested with fear in his voice.

"I don't know! I just assumed it would be a straight shot after getting inside!" Amelia yelled, clearly annoyed at the situation.

"Never that easy," Piped in Larriott with a gruff yet odd voice as he stared off to the hallway they had come down initially.

The group of would-be ship thieves could hear loud talk coming back from where they entered. The guards were clearly surprised by a new door, and they obviously would not have let kids sleep in that alley if they had known about it being there. As the group stared back in the direction they had traveled, it dawned on Jason that they only had one option. They had to pick a direction and run.

Pushing past the other three, Jason yelled quietly, "Quick, we have to go!"

Amelia leaped forward and replied sternly, "This way, then!"

Amelia took off running towards the path to her left, and the boys, Jay and 3T followed behind swiftly. After about a dozen steps, the alarms in the building started. Loud sirens and flashing yellow lights accompanied the group as they ran. They arrived at another split in the hall. One way stayed straight, and the other turned to the right. Jason had fallen behind in the mad sprint down the hall and was already twenty steps behind Amelia, who decided to keep the group fleeing straight, when he got to the turn off. That was very fortunate for Amelia and 3T.

When Jason got to the hall split, Amelia was at the end of the hall, and 3T was halfway between the two. Amelia was about to jerk open the door at the end when it burst open on its own accord. Three more guards came flying out the door!

"I've found the intruders, try to restrain! They are all kids. One of them is De... Ugh..."

By the time those words had escaped his mouth, Amelia had delivered a strong left jab to the guard's throat hard enough to cause the next words to turn into gasps for air. The hopeful captain turned to run.

Amelia shouted, "Run back the way we came!"

3T did not need to be told twice, as he quickly turned and started back towards Jay. The youngest of this trio, Jason, had darted to the path to his right as soon as the door had burst open. This path was much shorter, only a few steps. At the end, the path split again. However, the split led to a set of stairs on each side. Most importantly, the stairs were labeled. One heading up, labeled 'Office', and one heading down, labeled 'Hangar.'

Jason turned around just in time to make it back to the original path to grab 3T to stop him from sprinting back by.

"This way!" Shouted Jason.

"Good as any, I guess!"

With an angry voice, Amelia yelled, "I said back the way we came! Oh, crud!"

Laser blasts, from the end of the hall, where Jay had initially warned them that they had already been caught on to about the break-in, zipped past Amelia's head. If they had followed her plan, they would have been trapped. She, having quickly lost her reluctance, followed the two boys.

While gesturing to his friends to go down to the hangar to the right, Jason, having a very clever thought, yelled at the top of his lungs so the guards that were about to fill the hall could hear, "Hurry, up to the office!"

The trio quickly started down the stairs to the hangar. Luckily, they were fast enough for them to not be seen in which direction they had gone. That distraction gave the kids just enough time to make it over half way down the ten flights of stairs before the guards realized they had been duped and started after them in the correct direction. The door to the staircase the trio had rushed down burst open even more violently than the one that surprised Amelia earlier!

"There they are!" One guard yelled as he came bursting through.

The would-be ship thieves were already almost at the bottom of the stairs, though. Amelia was the first to get to the bottom door. She rammed straight into it, expecting it to fly open. She bounced back, though! The door was locked.

Amelia reeled and started shouting, "No, no, no, no, no, no!"

3T shouted, "Get back, I've got this, Captain A!"

"Mister Tymes, what do you mean?"

Without saying another word, Timolas Thomas Tymes pushed past Amelia and pulled a strange tool from his pocket. Jay had seen him pull it out a few times in the last few weeks and was always impressed by it. 3T held an E-Class laser knife in his hand.[8] He unfolded a short, thin point from the knife and hit the button to send swathes of energy out from that protrusion. 3T then stabbed the laser knife into the door lock and jerked the handle. With ease, the door flew open!

"How'd you know to do that?" Amelia asked, dumbfounded at how easily a lock guarding a space ship could be broken.

"I learned from my big…"

"Later!" Yelled Jason as he pushed his buddy and the mysterious girl through the door.

The guards had gotten within three flights of stairs by the time they made it through the door. Jason was the last through the door, and, because of that, he was the last to see the massive spaceship that Amelia had told them of.

The ship was a matte red with gold highlights. It looked similar to an airplane, except the wings were further back and it was large enough where you could imagine around a dozen people could live inside comfortably for months. It, also, did not look very aerodynamic. It had triple thrusters, one under each wing and one connected at the back to the main engine. Each wing also had a turret connected on top where it joined the main body of the ship.

Windows were tinted over, preventing anyone from seeing inside the ship from the outside, but they gleamed in the warehouse light, as did most of that pristine vessel at that time. Even the unadventurous Jason thought it was beautiful. He might even have wanted to get on it if he had any sense of adventure.

However, the trio had no time to stop and admire the ship. The guards had been quickly gaining on them! They were almost at the ship, though! They could make it on board and close the ramp behind them! Except, the ramp… The ramp was not down. They had no way to climb on board. The kids made it to where the ramp should be and realized this very unfortunate truth.

They stopped.

Amelia seemed to have lost that bravado and air of confidence she had as she realized her ticket to escape had disappeared. 3T had tears start to form in his eyes as he realized his best hope to go to space had vanished. Jay lowered his head in shame because he had failed to keep someone else he cared about safe.

The guards closed the ground between them and the kids and realized this for themselves before one of them spoke up.

"Alright kids, the chase is over. Put your hands up and surrender without a fight."

"Yes, of course. You caught us," Amelia barely choked out. It was hard to tell what emotion she was trying to hold back.

The kids started to put their hands behind their heads, and the guards started forward when, without warning, the ship thrusters fired on! The guards that were not yet directly under the ship had to retreat before the heat burned them. The two guards under the ship already, one being the guy who had his throat punched in earlier, rushed forward in hopes of subduing the teens. Amelia, having been shocked out of her hopeless stupor by the ship coming alive, seemingly on its own, stepped towards the charging guards. Before either had a chance to grab anyone, the soon-to-be captain kicked one hard enough in the head to instantly knock the poor guy out cold!

The other guard saw what had just happened and, having been punched in the throat earlier, stopped short and raised his N-Class rifle. Jay and 3T, however, had already flanked the man. They both started yelling as loud as they could, causing the guard to lose his focus on Amelia. That was a horrible, awful, dreadful mistake for the guard. Amelia acted in his hesitation and managed to disarm the man in one swift move. That poor guard, being held at laser point by three kids, realized he should have stayed home that day.

The ship, almost sensing that the fight was at a pause, lowered its ramp for its future inhabitants. The kids, wasting no time, rushed up the ramp! This gangplank to safety led up into the base of the ship, where the kids discovered an area that seemed to be a kind of workshop. Tools and scrap and spare parts and machines covered in tarps were all over the place. In this space, the trio also found a horrifying sight: Larriott! He was as disturbing as ever.

"Took you kids long enough. Should have just went down the stairs instead of sprinting down that hall," Larriott chortled.

"Mister Larriott, please close the door and get us out of here."

"Aye, Captain."

Larriott hit a switch that caused the ramp to start to fold back up under the ship. The old man then started off, up some stairs, past a few doors, around a very nice looking chair, and towards the front of the ship to what would be a cockpit on a plane. The kids followed after, not knowing what to do to help. A moment later, they arrived at the 'cockpit', called a pilotrest on a ship such as this.

The pilotrest was a 15 by 15 foot room with hundreds of gauges, meters, buttons, and switches. There were four chairs in the room, one on each side of the cabin and two facing out, like pilot seats on a plane.

Larriott hit a few buttons and about a dozen switches without looking up while working his way to the front seats. Larriott finally sat down, pulled a steering device from the floor up towards himself, and looked back at the kids.

"Ya might want to sit down, crew."

Amelia and 3T rushed to the chairs on each side of the room. Both were very nervous of being in that room as the ship was about to take off for the first time. Jason Calloway, however, delayed as he realized that meant he had somehow found himself on an adventure and a part of a ship's crew. That small delay left only one seat in the room available. The one at the front. The one facing out towards space. Jason slowly took that seat while 3T looked on, shocked that he did not think to sit there first.

The teens fastened their seatbelts. The engines started to ignite and the ship tipped upwards. The ceiling above them spread open. Pure darkness ahead. No stars, due to the light from the city. Jay stared forward, looking up into a void. The ship started to rise forward towards that abyss, rising above the building, upward. Jay looked out of the side of the window and barely glimpsed at his alley. A home he would never know again, but the ship went on, upward. The ship crashed through several floating walkways as it moved still upward. Past the clouds and the tallest of buildings, upward. The stars started to pop into view as this ship, with those three kids, each with different outlooks on life, went upward.

Amelia turned towards Jason and said, very smugly, "Welcome to the crew. You made a pretty good lookout, kid."

Before Jason processed these words, the ship flashed upwards and onwards into space.

Chapter 3: Things to See

The ship only took a minute to reach the edges of Earth's atmosphere. It was less than five by the time they passed the Moon. 3T stared at it as they went by. He had yet to see but one thing more beautiful.[2] He loved moons. Amelia sighed in relief as she realized that all of her planning had succeeded. She was leaving her old life behind. Jay was still coming to terms with entering space.

Jason thought, *what is a no good kid like me going to do in space?*

It never occurred to him that the answer to that question was more than either 3T or Amelia could even imagine.

A few moments after passing the Moon, the ship began to become more steady. They were officially about to leave Earth's orbit. Some for the last time, though I do not want to spoil anything yet. Larriott, never looking away from space except to check his instruments and never blinking, sighed in relief of finally being back in space.

"Alright, kids, Captain, feel free to unfasten and explore the ship. I would recommend, Captain, that you three decide roles on and off the ship, such as a schedule of who is going to cook, and start to do an inventory of what we have and what we need to pick up on Mars. I've got to stay here while inside a solar system."

3T quickly unstrapped, popped out of his chair, and exclaimed, "Mars!? The real Mars? You have to be kidding, I think I died in that hallway."

"Thank you, Mister Larriott. Yes, Mister Tymes, our first stop will be Mars." Getting out of her seat, Amelia said in a commanding voice, "You two, follow me."

Jason, without saying a word, unbuckled and followed his new captain. 3T was already right beside her, though, asking about everything they passed. Amelia knew most of the answers to his questions, but even she did not seem to know everything.

They entered the Main Deck of the ship after leaving the pilotrest. The main deck had plenty of equipment for sensing space debris or nearby ships. The middle of the room had a holo-projector coming from the floor, but also, it looked like it could function as a table. Moreover, the room had a very comfortable looking captain's chair, which Amelia only glanced at for a moment.

"This is the main deck. For the most part, we can run ship diagnostics from here. We can, also, plot new courses, file information on discoveries, and help detect incoming threats from here. We will help Larriott man the shield functions, input the new travel courses, operate the forward stationary cannon, and even help co-pilot the ship from the pilotrest. Larriott will basically live in there, though, because that is his happy place."

"So, Captain, we will be making discoveries?" Asked 3T.

"Yes, I wish to have an adventure. As far from Earth as possible. To do that, we will inevitably have to make discoveries and take on odd jobs to make money, especially outside of Ultorian space," Replied Captain Hush.[10]

"That sounds swell, especially the part about making money. I only have 3 Earth credits."[11]

"I only have 0.5 UC," chimed in Jason.

Amelia, surprised one of the boys had any UC, asked, "Oh, you have an UC card then?"

"Yeah, I was given one when I started work in the salt mine a couple years ago."

With fluster on her face for just a moment, Amelia stated in a very matter-of-fact manner, "Yes, De Salina does pay everyone in UC. Must have been a big mine. Are you not a bit young for that though? Working in a mine?"

"Well, yeah, my foster parents were arrested after someone reported them. I worked there for over a year. Only cash I kept was from my last month's pay. 3 UC."

3T chimed in, "Yeah, Da Salina and his whole family can kiss my ass. He bought my family's land after he discovered a loophole in our lease agreement. The family got almost nothing and the bank got millions. We lost the largest dairy farm in the Virginia's."

Looking down, Amelia continued, "Yes, I have heard a hundred stories like that. Let us focus on the ship for now though, please. Come along."

They continued out of a door behind the captain's chair and entered into a wide hallway that had two doors on either side and three on the end, two of which were smaller than the one in the middle. Amelia strided over to the door on her left, which, if that were a sea ship, would be the starboard side. She waved her hand in front of a door and it opened into a medium sized room with four metallic crates and some wall lockers.

Amelia smiled, "Ah, yes. This must be storage."

"What's in the crates?" 3T asked.

"I do not know, yet. Let us find out."

Amelia walked over to one crate and undid a locking mechanism on the top by holding down a large button. The lid on the crate popped open on some hinges on the back. The boys looked over each of Amelia's shoulders to see what the opening lid would reveal. They all knew immediately that they were in luck. The crate was full of hundreds of water crystals, large enough that two or three would fit into the palm of an average human hand.[12] These crystals could sustain a twelve human crew for years, if not a full decade.

"That is amazing! I've never seen so many water crystals," 3T mused.

"Yeah, these are worth probably 10UC a piece. There looks to be roughly a 1,000 here," Jason said while doing the basic math in his head.

"10,000, Mister Calloway. Antonio De Salina did have access to more freshwater than anyone else on the planet. Let us check the other three crates. I have a feeling we have other valuable resources here."

"That's 123,280 gallons," Jay said quietly to himself.

3T was the one to move on to the next crate, and he pushed the middle button the same way he had seen Captain Hush do a few moments before. The crate opened the same way as the one before. However, this time, the trio of teens saw little, multicolored orbs instead of crystals, all sorted in trays based on color. Amelia looked confused.

"I do not actually know what these are, gentlemen."

3T and Jason looked at each other and back at Amelia and said in unison, "Food orbs."[13]

"Food orbs?"

"You've never seen a food orb?" Asked Jason.

"No, I have not. How do you two know about them?"

"Well," started 3T, "Most foods that need to be preserved are stored in them. Each orb can have any kind of food in them, from loaves of bread to bushels of apples to a whole cattle worth of steak. Already cooked. It was their rise in popularity that made *Mama Mack's* a household name."

"Yeah, it makes it easy for families to buy in bulk, preserve foods, and speed up the cooking process. They brought the price of food way down."

"Oh," Amelia said without thinking for a change, "I guess, I just have not had much experience with having to provide food for myself."

3T stared at Amelia, "You really need to tell us who you are, Cap."

"Yes, and I will, in time. Maybe. Just know that I lived a very," Amelia looked visibly distressed as she continued, "Pampered life. However, back to the task at hand, how do we know what is in each orb."

Jason pulled a piece of paper from one side, "It looks like we have a list. Each red orb has meat enough for a crew of 8. Each Yellow has 10 loaves of bread. Each Blue has produce, fruits and vegetables, that could feed 10 humans."

"Wonderful, it looks like we have food, then," Captain Amelia stated as she moved to the next crate, wanting to keep moving on.

She followed the same process, as before, to open the third crate. It opened like the others. This crate revealed something that lit up Amelia's face like nothing before it had. There were four containers, each marked S-Class.

Amelia knew, immediately, what they were and turned to say, excitedly, "These are S-Class laser knives! I say knives, but they are more like swords! They are powerful enough to cut through real steel swords!"

The captain was clearly excited.

"Alright," Amelia started before she cleared her throat, and as Jay and 3T each pulled a sword box out from the crate. "Crew, I doubt you have been trained to fight. I plan on teaching you the basics of combat. As you saw, I am proficient at fighting. I have mastered karate, judo, fencing, and boxing. We will get practice swords on Mars. For now, let's see what kind of blades these knives form."

3T chuckled as he thought this drop in formality from his new captain was hilarious. Even Jason smiled a little at her excitement. Amelia started to pull out a box the same as Jay and 3T already had.

Jason whispered to 3T as they started to open the boxes to reveal the blades, "She must really like stuff like this. She used a conjunction."

"I know," 3T whispered back. "I think I kinda like this crazy lady."[14]

Jay raised an eyebrow and teased, "She's a lady now, huh?"

Before 3T could reply, Amelia, having ripped her box open first, pulled her laser blade from its case, one made from cherry wood. Without noticing the blushing Timolas, the captain held her blade out. Initially, it was just a normal looking handle. She pressed an activation button and a long curved rod, about 26 inches long shot from the handle. The rod ignited to reveal a dark red and purple pulsing katana.

Amelia, amazed at the blade, could not hide her emotion on her face. She was truly happy. Like a child who got a puppy for the first time.

"I always wanted one of these. I was even jealous of your little E-Class knife, Mister Tymes."

"I'm glad you are happy," 3T stated as he pulled his little knife out, turned it on to its lowest setting, and broke the seal on his box that was giving him trouble.

3T looked at the case he had chosen from the crate. That case was a dark stained oak. He opened the latch and then the case's lid to reveal a very short but thick, black metal handle.

"Oh, it's a bit thick," 3T said as he pulled it from the case.

"That is because that is actually two blades," Amelia explained. "Look, they come apart."

3T pulled the two handles apart just as Amelia showed him. He took a step back, held each handle to each of his sides, and hit the ignition. A short 12 inch rod popped out from each handle and immediately began to glow a light green, with a touch of pulsing yellow near the rods, in the shape of daggers.

"Neat, same color as my knife," 3T stated as he turned the daggers back off and watched as the rods quickly retracted back into the handles. "What's in your case, Jason?"

Jay, who had his box open for a bit already looked down at his case, a very light maple wood. The young boy, who had never held a weapon except for K-Class laser picks in the salt mine, nervously opened the case. Inside he saw a handle much more finely crafted than the katana and the twin daggers. This handle had a leather wrapped handle, a ruby pommel, and an inscription across the golden cross guard that read 'VADE INVENIAT PACEM.'[15]

Jason pulled the beautiful handle from the box to show to his two friends.

"Mister Calloway, that is an Attorium brand laser blade,"[16] Amelia said, shocked. "That blade is worth well over 30,000UC! Go on, let us see the blade!"

"Yeah, Jay, that thing is special! My brothers and I always talked about those blades! We all agreed none of us would ever see one though. Go on, light it!"

Jason, feeling pressured, uneasily, held the handle out and hit the ignition switch. A rod, 40 inches long, sprang out from the middle of the cross guard. Immediately, the rod burst into flames! The blade, now the shape of a claymore, glowed a golden, beautiful yellow, and, every few seconds, a red flash of lightning zapped its way along the blade. All three teens stood speechless.

Jason turned the blade off and watched it retract the rod the same as the daggers and katana had done. Jay then put the handle back in its case and started to put the case back in the crate. Amelia swiftly stopped him.

Amelia, thinking about Jason working in a salt mine, looked him in the eye and told him, "You are to keep that blade. It is yours, a gift from me to thank you for helping me steal this ship. I will train you to use it in time."

Jason was blown away, 30,000UC could buy ten mansions, "What? Keep it? This thing could pay 600 salt miners wages for a year! 900 if they were kids."

"You could sell it, but you will probably need it here in space. Pirates and monsters do exist."

"I'll kick his butt if he sells that thing!" 3T interrupted. He clearly would not let the dream weapon be sold without a fight.

"Then one of you take it," Jason argued.

"Nah, I've got daggers in my favorite color."

"You deserve that weapon. You more than earned it," Amelia praised. We would have been caught twice over in that warehouse. Also, I am trained in using katanas more so than longswords."

"Well, what about the last box, that blade would probably suit me better," Jay offered.

"No, Mister Calloway. You have your weapon. End of discussion. The last blade can go to whoever loses their weapon first or to our first new crewmate."

"Wait," interrupted 3T. "What about Larriott?"

"Mister Larriott is a pacifist. He might line up a shot for you while piloting, but even then someone will have to shoot in his place. A blade would be useless to him."

"You guys are weird, Captain. Let's open the last crate,"
3T said before Amelia could argue otherwise. "Here, Jay, you open
this crate, it is only fair."

"Yeah, sure," Replied Jason as he sat his new laser blade
case down.

Jay moved over to the last crate. He pushed the button the
same way he saw Captain Amelia and Timolas Thomas do before.
This time, the crate remained shut.

"Looks like this only has a key lock," Amelia stated
looking over Jason's shoulder. "Can you unlock this, Mister
Thymes?"

"Yes, but it will destroy the lock."

"All the better. Locks are oppressors."

"Weird. Alright, Jay, hold the button to open it while I fry
the lock,"

Jason pressed the lock the same way he had earlier. 3T
pulled his E-Class knife back out. He ignited it on the lowest

setting and then shoved it straight into the lock and twisted. Like magic, the crate started to open to reveal the cargo that needed even more security. All three kids were shocked by what they saw: a pile of scrap.

"It's just junk?" Asked Jason.

"I think so," replied Amelia, confused.

"Actually, it looks like parts," said 3T.

"Parts to what?" Asked Amelia.

"It's a broken robot!" Exclaimed Jay.

"It is!" Said both 3T and Amelia together.

All three kids had seen robots. Jay worked with several in the salt mines. 3T had seen a few on the dairy farm that helped milk the cows and do more extraneous work. Amelia had seen all kinds of robots, from ones used to cook and clean to the ones used to fight wars. So, a robot was not very exciting. However, a robot, even broken, is twice as exciting as some broken parts and ten times as exciting as a pile of junk.

"Interesting, we will have to get this thing fixed," Amelia said as she was losing interest. "We can take it down to the workshop, where the ramp opens and closes at, to work on it."

"Makes sense," 3T replied.

"Good, we will do that later," Amelia stated as she moved to the lockers. "Let us check the lockers and move on."

Amelia pulled open the first locker. Jay and 3T pulled open the second and third immediately after. All three teens were greeted to the same sight. Three outfits, a bag of health care supplies, a G-Class laser pistol, and an H-Class laser rifle.

Amelia pulled the rifle from her locker, "Look, we have even more weapons. We should be able to defend ourselves and even dispatch pirates with these."

3T, listening to the talk of the rifles and pistols, pulled a white uniform with golden trim from his locker, "These look like they are made from Exclon.[17] All of the stories about space mention them. These things can stop up to H-Class lasers. I guess they would protect from friendly fire, huh?"

Looking over at 3T holding the white uniform up from his locker, Jason started to examine the red and black uniforms in his locker to see they are all made from Exclon, a very protective fabric.

Jason pulled the bag of health care supplies from the locker, "3T, we have soap, tooth brushes, and deodorant. We need these much more than lasers."

Both Amelia and 3T looked at Jay in shock that he was not impressed by lasers and uniforms before the captain stated, "He is not wrong. You gentlemen need a shower. Bad."

3T, sticking the uniform back in the locker, sighed before saying, "Yeah, living in an alley does cause one to forget to shower."

"I'm sure Amelia will show us where we can get clean, shortly. Let's check out the other rooms."

"Right, Mister Calloway, let us move on."

Amelia led the boys out of the room and opened the door across the hall. The door slid open to reveal some kind of lab. There were all kinds of medical equipment in that room. Scanners, pods, microscopes, tools of all kinds.

"This is the medical bay and science lab. I have only a basic knowledge of these things. That pod is a replenish pod; it will help heal minor wounds. That scanner table thing can scan for diseases of all kinds and if we have a medical professional operate it, it can perform surgery to replace body parts. These," Amelia picked up a tool that looked like a laser pistol, "Can implant special chips in us. Like our translator chips."[18]

"Our translator chips?" The boys asked together.

"Oh, you probably do not have one, yet. We will need to implant the two of you with translator chips that will fuse to your brains and allow you to understand almost all alien languages without a delay."

"Does it hurt?" Asked Jason.

"Very much."

"Do we have to?" Asked 3T.

"Yes, but we will do that after we leave the solar system. You will need a day or week of rest afterwards, crewmen."

Jay and 3T frowned at each other, but they still followed behind Captain Hush as she led them from the lab and to the triple doors at the end of the hall.

"The starboard door is the stairs; we came up those an hour back now, if you remember. The door on the other side is an elevator. This middle door," Amelia pressed the button to open the door and continued, "Is the engine room."

The door opened to reveal a very large room, spanning the near 30 foot height of the ship. The room contained a massive machine, slick and also complex. It had tubes that glowed a blood red that bathed the room in that horrifying color. The drive hummed a very low hum, but the trio could tell there was another sound that was far too high pitched for any human's, or even dog's, ear to hear. It was not wise to spend too long in that room while the ship was gliding through space. The kids each approached and looked down to see another floor below them. The room would impress even the oddest of souls.

"This is our Solar Drive.[19] It is a very new model. It is able to warp us faster than light but only in space between star systems. Something about pulling us into a dimension where space is not as large. This model can get to Mars in 20 hours, when it is an average distance away, of course. We should probably hire an engineer at some point."

"This is amazing," 3T awed.

"It is," Jason replied, recognizing that he also felt the amazement of the room. "Will we get an engineer on Mars too?"

"Maybe, it depends on our luck, but I doubt we will, Mister Calloway."

"Can you call me something else? The way you say it reminds me of my jerk of a dad."

"I apologize, Mister," Amelia paused and sighed for a moment, "Jason. I had no idea it was offensive. What happened with your dad?"

"He left. Never came back."

"Ah, well, that is too bad. I think I understand the feeling. Don't worry, Mister Jason, I do not plan on letting you be left again. That is a captain's duty."

Jay smiled a little, but did not say anything. He looked down at the large engine filling the room and wondered if Amelia meant those words. The captain did, but he did not know that yet.. He knew that he did feel a little glad that 3T did not leave him, even if it meant having to go on something as wild as a trip into space. His friend put his arm around the boy's shoulders.

"We got another floor to explore, friend. *Let us move on,*" 3T said in a voice trying to imitate Amelia's own.

"You are not very good at impressions," Amelia stated coldly, but with an air of humor, while turning away from the boys.

Chapter 4: A Place to Live

The two friends followed the new captain out of the engine room and barely made it into the elevator with her as she always walked very fast. Amelia pressed the button to go to the middle floor. The elevator moved, as elevators do, down a floor. The door opened and revealed the final floor the teens had yet to have seen. The hallway before them was much like the one from the floor above, except the door on the other end of the hall was nonexistent. The teens saw straight into a room that had couches, screens, tables, and many other amenities that a crew would enjoy.

The boys were very impressed with this room. They moved into that space first, before Amelia. 3T sat on one of the couches, before remembering he was kinda filthy, and stood up. Jason looked around the room and noticed that the room was stocked with many different board and card games, both digital versions and the old fashion versions that were first played many years, centuries even, before. Amelia turned on the largest screen and a news broadcast from Earth came on immediately:

"Today was a great day at the stock markets. Salina Industries hit another record high, mere days after announcing plans to build a new system of high speed earthbound travel that will begin construction in Neolandia and travel all the way to New Mars. This new line of travel will ease the commute time of thousands of people who are terrified of using teleporting technologies. It will turn a few hours journey into less than 30 minutes. Mama Mack's Distributions have also risen to heights after announcing a new wave of improved food orbs. In other news, the Ultorian Empire has promised to supply anyone on Earth or its colonies with translator chip implants at no to little charge. These chips should increase the job market for millions, as they will allow anyone to understand alien languages. It will make traveling to the other parts of the Empire a reality for millions.

Finally, we will end with some bad news, the daughter of Antonio De..."

Amelia flipped the screen back off and said sternly to the boys, "The door on the starboard side back in the hallway is the baths. There are several private showers, toilets, and a public spa tub. There is also a washing system for your clothes in that public space. The two of you, go get cleaned up. It is very late. Put on those uniforms, at least until your clothes are cleaned or until we get you some new clothes on Mars. Meet back here when you are done, and we will finish the tour with your rooms. I am going to check on my quarters and figure out how to use the kitchen while you are doing that. Dismissed."

"Yes, Captain," The boys said together, grateful for the chance to get clean.

"Don't explore too much without us, Captain," 3T added as he ran towards the stairs. "Race, Jay, stairs versus elevator."

Jason, even though he was still contemplating the happenings of the day and the information he gleaned from the news, took off towards the elevator, knowing that 3T needed the challenge.

Jason did lose the race and even the rematch to the showers but just by a moment each time. He did not much mind losing, especially since he could not make the elevator speed up, but he knew that next time he would call the stairs or hope 3T got distracted on his way up. It took Jay and 3T nearly an hour to get clean. They took very long, hot showers powered by a water crystal large as a very giant man. 3T cleared his mind as he stood under the hot water. He was thinking about how great that was. Jason, on the other hand, considered his new place in life, the lookout on a crew that just stole Earth's richest person's spacecraft, as he sat on the floor under the hot, flowing water of his own shower.

Getting their teeth brushed with A-Class laser tooth brushes was wonderful for them. The ones they had in the alley were not very good, as they did not have many means to keep them clean. Even Jason felt like he could get used to having a home like this ship. The two teens obviously also horse-played just a bit before finally putting on their Exclon outfits. Jason picked a white uniform and 3T picked the black, to meet back up with Amelia in.

While the boys were getting clean, Amelia checked out her quarters, located directly on the far end of the living area where the group separated. Her quarters were obviously lavish. Large, princess style four post bed, a very neat writing/work desk, and her own private bath all filled her new space. This room was meant for Antonio De Salina. So, it was designed for the richest of the rich. Amelia left the room on the other side that she entered from. That door led back into the pilotrest with a door opening beside the stairs leading back up to the main deck.

Amelia smiled as she watched Larriott steer the ship through the emptiness of space. The old, mysterious man seemed more at peace than she had seen him ever before. Amelia continued up the stairs and into the main deck. She looked at the captain's chair, longingly.

Not yet, she thought.

Amelia moved back through the door to the hall, just in time to see the boys disappear back down on their race to the shower. Amelia was glad she invited these two with her. She hated the idea two kids were living in an alley, especially when she thought of the home she had abandoned. She moved into the storage room after the sounds of the boys had disappeared with them.

Amelia looked at the broken robot and thought about how odd it was to be in that room, in that crate. Everything else was for survival, but the robot just seemed out of place. The captain collected the cases containing the laser blades that the trio had left behind. She, also, picked out the red uniform for herself from the locker she opened earlier and grabbed a couple of food orbs. She left the room, arms full, and moved to the elevator.

Once back on the middle floor, Amelia took the boys' blades to the rooms on each side of her own and left them on the beds, one for each of them. Those rooms were also very fancy, but not nearly as extravagant as her own. She then proceeded to go back to her room and took a very quick shower herself and changed into the red uniform. The boys were still showering, or horse-playing, which gave Amelia plenty of time to figure out how a food orb worked.

The kitchen was located across the hall from the showers, and it was stocked with all kinds of goods. Amelia found a manual in one drawer that explained the way food orbs in the oven were supposed to be used. It took her several tries, but Amelia eventually got a red and yellow orb to expand into several roasted chickens and several loaves of bread. The oven only took a minute to prepare all of that food. She took the food to the living area and sat it down on the dining table. The captain also sat three bottles of De Salina brand Solar Water she gathered from the kitchen on the table. She then took a plate of food to Larriott, and then she returned to wait on the boys.

The boys were pleasantly surprised at the food. They also thought that it was funny that they all picked different colored suits. The trio sat together and ate the meal Amelia had prepared as she explained the kitchen to them. However, they got full quick, as they swallowed food faster than a human should be able to.

"I am tired, gentlemen. I know you are, too. I did witness how early you two rose this morning to go about your day. Mister Jason, your room is on the port side. Mister Tymes, the starboard."

"Aye, aye, Captain," 3T stated as he got up from the table. "See you in the morning. Night, Jay."

"Goodnight, 3T," Jason said to his friend while turning towards Amelia. "Thank you for the food, Amelia."

Amelia smiled again as 3T's door shut behind him, "Don't let 3T hear you not call me captain. He still hasn't figured out I have no idea what I am doing."

"He is a little slow, sometimes," Jason said with a smile. "But he means well, I think, and no one really ever knows what they are doing."

"Yes, I think so. Now, let's go to sleep, kid. Mars is a fast paced place, and we have a lot to do."

"Goodnight, Captain."

"Goodnight, Jay."

The two new friends parted for their rooms. Jason entered his new abode and saw the case at the end of his bed. He was still nervous about the weapon. He collapsed onto the bed anyway though. Jay stared up at the ceiling and wondered how a kid that did not even want to live could go on an adventure in space.

However, he did drift off to sleep, since a soft bed on a spaceship will always beat a pile of rags in an alley.

Chapter 5: The First Morning

It would have been a little before 4AM back on Earth when Jason opened his eyes. Jason never really slept more than six hours a night. He prefered to get his rest with naps in the middle of the day. This morning, like many others, Jason laid in bed looking up. However, the last few months Jay laid on a pile of old sheets and rags that he had stolen from dumpsters and stared up through cracks in the cover of his alley and gazed upon the sky. Today, Jason laid in a bed staring up at the ceiling of a spaceship. A spaceship destined to explore that same sky that he looked up at only the previous morning.

Jason stared for an hour at this ceiling. He initially thought the previous day was a dream, but the longer he stared, the more he understood that he was flying through space. He was flying away from where his mother had died. He was flying away from where his father abandoned him. He was flying away from where he was forced to work in a salt mine. Away from an abusive foster family. Away from a pile of rags that he called a bed. Away from a world that had destroyed him.

Jason thought about all of those things. He thought about how he blamed himself for his misfortune. He thought about how he would end up ruining 3T's and Amelia's life. However, he also thought about finding food. Then he remembered they had plenty. They had plenty of food, the ship was not a filthy alley, but the dishes were still dirty. That thought gave him enough motivation to finally get up out of bed. He needed to wash the dishes.

Jason stood up from the bed. He realized that he had got the bed a bit messed up. He had forgotten to take off his old shoes when he laid down the previous night. He swept the grime off the cotton sheets and made the bed. He looked at the maple case containing his new laser blade and sighed at the thought of ever needing such a thing. Jay started out of his room.

Jason found the living area empty. He looked at 3T's door and hoped he slept well. He would not be awake for a couple hours. Jay knew that 3T probably was restless last night in all of his excitement. The youngest member of the crew moved to the table and gathered a few of the plates and carried them off to the kitchen.

It was Jay's first time in the kitchen. He was impressed by the equipment in the room. The oven was state of the art, as you would expect from a trillionaire's ship. It could prepare food orbs in mere moments. Jason did not miss the fact that there were a few busted food orbs by the machine. It was not hard to guess it was Amelia who had messed up a few orbs while making dinner the night before. Jay went ahead and disposed of that trash and proceeded to place the dirty plates in a washing machine.

Jason left the kitchen to return for the rest of the dishes. Upon turning back into the living area, Jay was greeted by a surprising sight.

"Good morning, Mister Jason. I see you get busy quite early. I must not let my crew show me up," Captain Amelia Hush stated playfully as she gathered the other dishes from the table. "Larriott said we were making good time towards Mars. We are only nine hours away."

"Good morning, Captain," Jason replied as he started to help gather more dishes. "That's good. 3T will be very excited to make it there. He has always talked of going to the stars and other planets."

"I figured based on how excited he became from suggesting he join the crew," Amelia paused as she moved towards the kitchen. "I am sorry that I drug you into this as well. I hope you can be as happy on this ship as you were in that alley."

"That's alright, Captain. A bed is nice for a change. I haven't really had a bed in a while."

"Well, I would not know about that. I have not ever been without a bed," Amelia said as she entered the kitchen. "I have also never washed any dishes. Would you please show me how to use this machine?"

"Yeah, of course," Jay answered as he moved to a very sophisticated dishwasher. "We just put the dishes in and hit the green button. The machines are smart enough to wash, sterilize, and dry the dishes on its own."

Moments after pressing the button to start the machine, the machine dinged to let the teens know it was already finished.

"That was quick, Mister Jason."

"Most dishwashers aren't that fast. This ship has some state-of-the-art equipment. My foster family's dish machine took about five minutes."

"Foster parents? What happened to your real parents?"

"They are both gone. Mom died shortly after I was born. I don't even know her name. Father left, as I told you last night, and never came back," Jay replied with a sigh.

Amelia paused as she was putting the dishes away into the storage cabinets, "I'm sorry to hear that."

Jay sighed, "It's okay. Hey, let's get that robot down to the workshop when we finish this."

"Good idea, Mister Jason. Hmm, by any chance would you like to be the ship's robot expert? I, honestly, do not want to hire that many people."

"That is an idea, but I would probably just make things worse. Break things worse than they were to begin with," Replied Jason as the two teens moved out from the kitchen. "I also don't know anything about robots."

"Nonsense. You will easily pick up the skill," Amelia paused before finishing her thought as she saw 3T exit from the bathroom at the same time as the captain left the kitchen. "Good morning, Mister Tymes."

"Morning, Cap."

"Mister Jason and I were about to move the robot to the garage workroom."

"Wonderful, I would love to help with that."

"Come on, then."

"Race you," 3T shouted in a way to surprise Amelia as he took off towards the stairs.

Amelia, who turned red with anger at the idea of losing any competition, took off after 3T. Timolas had the head start, but Amelia would not be so easily defeated. 3T was already a few steps up the stairs when Amelia got there. However, the captain had many skills to utilize that 3T did not. She sprang forward and kicked off the wall. Amelia grabbed the guard rail up above her as she flew upwards and flipped over it and landed directly in front of 3T, on her feet. The boy was shocked that anyone could do such a thing. He even thought she might be alien with how she could do the things she did. Amelia smiled at him while they paused for a moment before she burst through the stairwell door to celebrate her victory. She was, however, shocked by what she saw when the door opened.

"That's a win for Jay," The lookout quipped as he stood by the door to the storage room.

"That is unfair, Mister Jason! You took the elevator!"

"Unfair? You just did a backflip up an entire flight of stairs! Who are you?" 3T asked as he followed Amelia into the hall.

"Haven't you figured it out yet, 3T?" Jay asked.

Amelia looked pale at these words, and Jason noticed.

"She's just a rich kid that had a lot of free time to learn some amazing skills, and now she just wants to make a name for herself on her own merit. Also, we proved yesterday the elevator was slower than the stairs."

Amelia was surprised at these words. She was almost afraid of what Jason had figured out about who she was. 3T had a look of understanding on his face as he accepted Jay's explanation.

"That makes sense, Jay. You are more clever than you look."

"Yeah, yeah. Let's get this bot moved. You will have time to explore the other crew quarters if we can get this done," Jay said as he turned away.

The boys entered the storage room as Amelia paused a moment in the hall to compose herself. She felt a bit annoyed at losing, a bit flustered that she accepted the race to begin with, and nervous that Jason might have known more than he let on. She breathed out and followed her crew inside. Jay and 3T were already examining the crate and trying to figure out how to carry something so big and full of metal parts. Amelia approached, but paused as she saw one of the rifles in the locker 3T had left open the previous night.

Amelia cleared her throat, "Boys, before we move that crate. I want to say something. Mister Jason, I believe you are too young to use or own a laser rifle without any previous firearm experience. The laser blade you were given will require days of training to use even in a simple way. The rifle, probably the pistol, as well, isn't something you should have, though. Mister Tymes and I probably should not have one either, but I am trained in the use of most weapons, and it is unfair if I have one and he does not since he is older than me. I will make him do a weapon safety course, however. When we have time, obviously. So, if it is alright, I will take your rifle. Again, I am very sorry, Mister Jason."

"That's fine, Captain. I don't really like weapons," Jason said unconcerned as he went back to examining the robot crate.

"I have actually been taught how to use firearms. Mainly hunting rifles, but I am a pretty good shot, none-the-less. Not as good as my older siblings, but still good," 3T explained to Amelia.

"Oh, alright then, Mister Tymes. All the better. Thank you, Mister Jason for understanding."

Amelia proceeded to move the rifle from Jay's locker to her own.

"I think I figured it out," 3T blurted suddenly while still fiddling with the crate.

"Yeah?"

3T pressed a button near the bottom of the crate and it started to float about half an inch up off the floor.

"Good job, Mister Tymes. I had no idea these things floated."

"We had something like this back on the farm. The crates we stored the milk cartons in floated just a bit. Though, they were a lot worse than these. Not as... hmm... sturdy, you know?"

"Yes, I think I understand," Amelia, not really understanding why the farm crates were not as strong as that one, said as 3T started to move the crate with ease towards and out the door.

As they approached the elevator, Amelia asked, "So, this farm, you had brothers? You mentioned them a couple times."

"Yeah, I have 11 siblings. 6 are older, 4 are younger. Only one sister."

Confused, Amelia asked, "That does not add up, Mister Tymes. What about the eleventh sibling."

"Yeah, I'm a twin," Replied 3T. "My twin stayed home to try and help my parents support the family."

"You say that as if your siblings were prone to leaving."

"Well, Onnar, Oscar, Sammy, and Franky were quadruplets and moved out at 18. Zed and Zeb were twins, one being the sister, about a year and a half older than me. Them, myself, and Tom…"

"Tom?" Jason interrupted, "Did you and your twin have the same name? You never told me his name."

"Yeah, he is Thomlas Timothy Tymes. My parents like similar names," 3T said as the elevator continued downward. "As I was saying, we got together and drew straws to see who had to stay and help the folks raise money and look after the young ones. My twin won. Zed and Zeb left the next day and I got a letter a year later saying that they had made it to space, working on a crew heading to New Pacifica.[20]

I left that day to follow in their footsteps. I had little success and two weeks later I was out of cash and was alone in Neolandia. That is when I met Jay. I do plan to return someday, though, you know? I miss my family more than anything. Especially the younger triplets: Bray, Lucas, and Ernic. I can do without the single born, Greymore."

Amelia thought about those words. Why did 3T's mother always give birth in multiples? Even more odd was the family struggling for money, but before she could ask a follow up, the elevator opened, and the boys moved the crate to one side of the workshop, away from the ramp. 3T pressed the button at the bottom again, and the crate gently touched down on the floor gently. Almost immediately, 3T was pulling tarps off of the machines in the room while Jason started to dig through the robot parts trying to find the head.

"Boys," Amelia mumbled before going to help remove the tarps

Most of the machines were for running diagnostics or to help perform repairs on the ship or any broken equipment. Several of the machines seemed like they would be able to lift larger objects up off the floor to help the person working on it to get underneath them. Under one tarp was nothing more than a cart for loading and unloading cargo. By the time 3T and Amelia were about to remove the last tarp, Jason had pulled the robot's head and torso from the crate and placed them on a hook designed for holding such things. He seemed to be a natural at figuring out any kind of puzzle, even the ones involving fixing a busted robot.

"Jay! Come look at this," 3T yelled as he stared at the machine under the last tarp.

Jason turned first to see the shock on Amelia's and 3T's face at what they uncovered. The lookout glanced past them to see some kind of bike. He knew immediately what it was, a brand new Yeanita Space Bike![21]

"De Salina really has everything," 3T said, dumbfounded.

"Yeah, these things cost over 100,000UC. I had an advertisement page for one. I always dreamed of saving up to buy one," Jay replied. "I guess that was my pipe dream like an Attorium blade was yours."

"Well, good and bad news, Mister Jason," Amelia smiled as she spoke. "Good news, the bike is as good as yours. Bad news, it is in pieces and you will have to learn to rebuild it if you wish to fly it."

"I guess I am going to have to learn to fix machines, too, then," Jay replied.

"Don't worry, Jay, I worked on plenty of farm equipment with my dad. We will get this fixed in no time!"

Maybe, Jason thought as pessimistically as ever.

"You will have plenty of time to work on it, crew," Amelia interjected. "It will take us around a month to get to the system we are traveling to after Mars. We will get plenty of spare parts for the bike and the robot while we are shopping later."

The boys replied simultaneously, "Yes, Captain."

Amelia barely hid her proud smile at them addressing her as captain together.

Chapter 6: Small Steps

The boys spent the next few hours tinkering on the space bike. Amelia stayed to watch for a while, but her interests did not involve learning more than she had to in mechanics. Amelia eventually went back up to the main deck. She examined the captain's chair, yet again, but still moved past it without sitting down. She entered into the pilotrest and smiled as she saw Larriott still steering the ship through the solar system. She sat in the seat beside the pilot and looked forward into space.

3T and Jason worked on the bike for a while, but they ultimately decided that they had no idea what they were doing. It was at that point that 3T left the workshop to explore the rest of the ship. He found himself turning right, starboard, down another hall before the living area. This hallway had five doors. The first door opened into a room that contained a very fancy inclosed chair and a bunch of buttons and controls. Timolas immediately guessed this had to be one of the manual turrets that he noticed back on the outside of the ship back at the warehouse. 3T saw no use in messing with something like that. So, he moved on. The other four doors all contained a small bedroom, each identical to each other, but much smaller than his own. He then moved on to the port side hallway to find that it was identical to the other one.

As Amelia talked with Larriott and 3T explored the ship, Jason took inventory of the tools in the workshop and sorted out the robot pieces from the crate. He was exceptionally tired and increasingly hungry. Jay went up to the kitchen and placed a yellow orb in the oven and a green orb under some running water. The yellow orb turned into four loaves of bread, while the green orb started to pop into dozens of fresh red apples. He immediately made four plates. First, he took two to the pilotrest for Amelia and Larriott. They both thanked him heartily. Next, he took a plate to 3T, who at this point was back in the living area, playing with a hatch that he had discovered that led up the main deck. Finally,

Jason sat at the table in the living area and ate three apples and an entire loaf of bread. It was not long after that he laid his head down upon the table and dozed off.

Jason usually did not remember his dreams from when he slept at night. However, the dreams that found their way into his mind during his daytime naps more easily stayed with him. This time, he dreamed of the days of his childhood. However, while he was running through the park, he came across a strange sight. A sword stuck in a stone. Moss had already overtaken the rock. However, as Jason approached, the young boy could make out every detail on the hilt of the sword. It was identical to the one that was on the laser blade that Amelia had given him the previous night. Jay cautiously approached the sword. He knew the stories of King Arthur. Only the rightful king could draw the blade from the stone. This younger version of Jason placed his hands around the handle, and, as he was about to pull, he was startled awake.

It was Larriott's raspy voice coming over an intercom system that had awakened him so suddenly.

"Good afternoon crew of the ship that has yet to be named. It is almost 1400 back where we are from back on Earth. We are starting the final approach to Mars. All crew needs to find a safe seat to strap into. I would recommend that Jay and 3T come up to the pilotrest so they can have the best view of their first touchdown on a new planet."

3T grabbed Jason from behind and pulled him up.

"You heard the magic voice from the ceiling! Hurry up! Let's get up there!" 3T yelled as he jerked Jay up.

Jason ran swiftly behind 3T, even that melancholy lad wanted to see Mars as they approached. Most children in those times dreamed of going to Mars and beyond at least a little bit. While Jay had no desire any longer to see those dreams fulfilled, he still remembered being a little kid wanting to go on an adventure. It seemed like a spark of wonder may have still been hidden deep down in the lad.

As the boys rushed into the pilotrest, they noticed Amelia sitting in the seat that she had occupied when they had left Earth.

"Gentlemen. Please take your seats. Mister Jason, opposite to me. I believe Mister Tymes deserves the chance to sit in the co-pilot seat to see our approach to Mars. I would also like for him to learn to pilot. I think he would enjoy that, and it would, eventually, lead to Mister Larriott being able to take a well deserved break."

"Thanks, Captain," 3T replied, not hearing anything after 'sit in the co-pilot seat.'

The boys sat in their respective seats and buckled in. The bright dot that was Mars started to become larger, even to the point you could make out the various colors from the surface of the planet. What was formerly the 'Red Planet' had been terraformed to have mass swathes of green foliage, and humans had used water crystal technologies, in more recent years, to form fresh water seas, lakes, and rivers that covered nearly a fourth of the planet. So, now, the surface of Mars was a mixture of greens, blues, and reds. Cloud cover was plentiful, as well, on that once barren planet.

"It's more beautiful than the pictures showed," Awed the enamored 3T.

The planet grew larger and larger as they approached. The two moons of Mars, strangely untouched by civilization, were on opposite sides of the planet.[22] The small moons were hard to make out at the angle the ship was traveling, but one was just coming around from behind the curvature of Mars while the other was already out to the side. Oh, 3T loved moons, including those two. It was not long before Larriott piloted the ship beyond these moons towards the surface of that beautiful planet.

That new world was unimaginable to Jason. Only the previous night, he had lived in an alley on Earth. Today, the teen was going to take his first step onto another planet. Amelia smiled as she saw the look on the boys' faces. She had felt the same the first time she visited Mars several years before. The captain was glad she decided to ask the boys to come with her. She thought they deserved the chance to adventure through space more than herself, and it was only fair since her actions would have had security eject the two kids from that filthy alleyway.

The ship slipped down into the atmosphere of Mars. The teens could now make out mountains, which were now capped with snow and valleys, now filled with fields of grass and flowers. Jay and 3T had both seen these things before, but never like they were from a spaceship flying boldly through the Martian sky. Amelia was even stunned at the breathtaking view.

Larriott looked back at the captain and started to speak to her.

"Ma'am, you're the captain. It is your duty to make the call to the port to ask for permission to land. You can delegate in the future, if you are busy, but that is ultimately your responsibility."

"Yes, of course, Mister Larriott," Amelia replied as if that was only a reminder. "Just to be clear, we need to land at the Blackfire Space Port with permission to stay for three days, even though we might not stay nearly that long, correct?"

"Yes, Captain. Though I recommend we don't stay but for a day. Blackfire is a terrible place."

Amelia turned her seat towards the instrument in front of her and activated what looked to be a very fancy radio. The captain changed the frequency to a number that appeared on a screen in front of the radio. The transponder powered on and a voice came through into the cabin.[23]

"This is Blackfire Space Port. State your business."

Amelia pressed a button and began to reply.

"This is Captain Amelia Hush of an yet unnamed custom flyer class vessel. We are seeking to land and park our ship for up to three days. Our intentions are to stock up on goods and supplies for a several month journey."

There was a pause before the voice on the radio came back in.

"We charge a docking fee of 4UC a day for flyers, another 4 for unnamed vessels. We will give your docking code upon initial payment."

Amelia pressed several buttons before pulling out her UC card and scanning it on a device beside her. She pressed a few more buttons before going back to the transponder.

"Blackfire, I have just sent over 24 UC to cover the full three days."

"Payment received, unnamed vessel. Proceed to Dock 0005. The docking code has been transmitted to your vessel."

Larriott turned to look at the captain and said, "Docking code received. Good job, Captain, but try to get a better deal in the future. They now know you have money and will probably pass on that info."

"Aye, Mister Larriott. Will do and thank you," Amelia said

as she turned to the boys. "Alright, we are stopping at the town Blackfire. In case you do not know, it is a very shady place. It is essentially a giant flea market and black market. Be on guard here. Mister Jason, you will stay with either myself or Mister Tymes while here. Mister Tymes, I will give you an F-Class laser pistol I found in a drawer in my quarters to carry with you. It is small enough to hide unlike the ones from the lockers."

Jay protested, "Why do I have to stay with one of you?"

"This place has a lot of thugs. You will not have a weapon. Your clothes will make you stand out. I am going to transfer a large sum of UC to you. So, all together, you would make for a really fine, easy target."

"She's right, kid," Larriott interjected as he began his approach to the town and before Jason could argue back. "I would also recommend that you put your regular clothes on over your Exclon uniforms. They aren't the style here."

"That's great," 3T said. "I actually finished washing Jay's and my own clothes while he dozed. Means I didn't do it for nothing."

"Good work, Mister Tymes. You will have to show me how to use those machines later," Amelia added praisingly.

The teens stopped talking as the details of Blackfire came into view. The town was much different from Neolandia. All of the buildings were low to the ground, and many looked like they might be mostly below the surface level. The buildings were vastly different, as well. Some were made of wood; others were clay. Small huts of steel that looked like repurposed spacecraft stood beside cloth tents. There was plenty of foliage in town, from mosses to grasses to small trees, but there were trails of red dirt all over. The teens could see the people down below. Many looked like they were out shopping, but even more of them looked like they were trying to peddle goods to these passers-by.

"You boys got lucky," Larriott said. "It looks like pad 0005 is on the ground level. Your first steps off the ship will be directly on the planet. Before any of you leave the ship, meet me in the med lab. You will all need a shot to prevent breathing in iron and to help with the change in gravity and atmosphere."

Jason sighed as he had not had a shot, or any medical treatment, in over five years. 3T felt the same, but he knew the importance of good health. The week after they met, 3T stole a couple of laser tooth brushes from a store just because he wanted Jay to start taking better care of himself, as well.

3T nearly bounced out of his seat with excitement as the ship started to hover over a very shoddy looking field that had the number 0005 painted on a sign just beside it. The ship started its final descent. Larriott hit a final button and the landing gear of the ship protracted out, and the ship touched down on its first foreign world.

All three teens bounded up immediately. Larriott was still powering down the ship as the kids were running out of the pilotrest. Amelia went through the door to her private quarters and started to put on the black clothes she had on the day before. She removed the laser katana handle from its case and fastened it to a clip on her side. She then pulled on her grey cloak to help keep her appearance hidden.

3T and Jason went down the hatch in the Main Deck that led to the living area. That is where Timolas had left their clothes. They were very raggedy, but Jay had stitched the damage back together in the alley quite often. Now clean, the clothes did not look nearly as bad as they had the previous night. They found themselves climbing back up to the Main Deck at the same time as Amelia and Larriott were coming in from the pilotrest. The crew moved into the med lab. 3T would not be quiet about how excited he was. Amelia hid her excitement, thinking that a captain should seem stoic. Jason was more anxious than anything. He wondered how something so wonderful would be ruined.

The three kids each winced in pain as Larriott gave them the shots. Each tried to act tough, but the shot was horrible. Moreover, Larriott knew just enough about administering them to make sure they hurt. Amelia was the only one to not have a tear from the pain, but she did say three times as many swears as the two boys did together. Larriott laughed and reminded her that he had a list of things that he needed, half of which were drinks a 15 year old should not be buying and very large quantities of Martian honey. Larriott refused to get the shot himself when it was his turn, mainly because it hurt, but also because he did not want to leave the ship.

The teens, all annoyed with the odd pilot, stormed off to the workshop. Amelia immediately hit a few buttons and the ramp lowered down to Mars's surface. The captain stood between the two boys. With Jay on her left and 3T on her right, the trio started down towards this new world. They all stopped together at the bottom of the ramp. Inches from Mars. Jason and Amelia both looked over at 3T.

"You first," Said the captain.

3T smiled back and replied, "No, together."

The three ship thieves were smiling as they, together, took their first small steps onto a new world.

Chapter 7: Luck on the First New World

The three teens had just stepped on Mars, a moment none of them would forget. 3T was beyond himself. His dream of visiting a new world had already come true. He knew he had to set bigger goals moving forward. Mars was just the start. There were millions of planets that support life, and most of them were still unvisited by intelligent life. Timolas Thomas Tymes wanted to visit as many as possible, rather that be 5, 50, or even 500.

Jason, too, was contemplating himself as he stepped onto Mars. He was just an orphan. He had no real talents, he thought. He wondered how a kid like him could have possibly been pulled into stealing a spaceship, how a kid like him could be standing on a new world, and how a kid like him could be called a crew mate on an adventure into the unknown. He tried his best to shake those thoughts off. Jay was on a new planet, and he was determined to make himself useful.

Amelia watched the two boys and they walked out from under the ship into the Martian sunshine. She remarked how the sky was more green now than the butterscotch like color it was only ten years ago, when she visited as a kid. The captain thought about how she came to Mars so long ago. She was so excited to see the planet. However, the part of Mars she stopped at that time was just a large city, and she was surrounded by her father's bodyguards the entire time. To her, it was just more Earth, just on a different planet. She let those feelings pass as she watched her new crew enjoy the novel world.

"Alright, boys," Amelia said as she pressed a button to close the ship's ramp. "We have a lot to do today. It is about 1500 where we are from, but it is midmorning here. We have plenty of time today to find all the things we need. However, first, we need to go to an Ultorian Credit service to get Mister Tymes an UC card."

"Why do I need a UC card?"

"So, I can pay you, Mister Tymes," Amelia paused as she looked around. "I have never been to this town, but most space ports have some kind of machine that can issue cards."

"There is one over there," Jason said, pointing off towards the town.

Both 3T and Amelia stared off in the direction he had pointed. It took a moment before either one of them saw the machine, a small panel attached to the side of a building that looked like it was for official business at the port.

"I'll be," Amelia started, impressed at Jason's attention to detail, before composing herself. "Yes, good eye, Mister Jason. Let us hurry up then."

As they started towards the UC machine, 3T spoke up, "So, how do you get a UC card?"

"Oh, Mister Tymes, it is rather simple. We can just register it in your name and the machine will fabricate a card in a few seconds."

"The captain is leaving out the point where the machine will poke you to get your DNA imprint," Jason added as he shuddered as he remembered getting his card.

"Yes, I forgot that part. My card belonged to my mother. So, I did not need to be pricked."

"I thought they are registered to only be used by their original owner?" Jay asked while 3T mumbled unhappily about having to be pricked again so soon.

"No, it is rather easy to add your children to an account. My father added me to my mother's account for my 10th birthday, mainly to keep her account open," They had just made it to the machine when Amelia said this.

3T stopped his mumbling as she said those words, "You haven't talked much about your family, so far. Who are they?"

"My mother, Emily, died when I was still little. My father and brother are absolute pricks. All you need to know, Mister

Tymes. Now, feel out your information and get pricked already. You do not have to use your real name."

3T started back with his mumbling, but he did start filling out his information on the screen. For his name, he chose to just put in his nickname. It only took him a few moments to get registered. At the end, the machine asked him, nicely, to place his palm on the screen to finish his account. Immediately upon touching the screen, a needle jammed into his palm and before he could even react to the sharp prick, the needle retracted back into the machine. 3T was still holding his hand in pain while the card was fabricated in a slot underneath the screen. Jason openly laughed at his friend, but Amelia turned away to hide her chuckle before recomposing again.

"Alright, crew," Amelia said as she turned around and 3T removed his new UC Card. "Hold out your cards and accept the deposits from my card. You will each be given 1,500 UC. 1,000 of which you are expected to use for the things we need for the ship, including your clothes, and the other 500 will be for whatever you want to use it on. Consider it a sign-on bonus."

The boys were speechless as they held up their cards. They wondered how rich that girl was exactly. As their cards flashed green and the captain's card flashed blue, the boys' jaws dropped as they saw the displayed balance on their cards shoot up to 1,500 UC.

"Thanks," the boys muttered out in disbelief and in unison.

"Spend it wisely. Mister Tymes," Amelia said as she moved right up against 3T as she removed an item from underneath her cloak and clipped it to his side, "Here is the laser pistol I mentioned earlier. Only for self defense, understood?"

3T blushed a little as Amelia pulled his tattered shirt down over the pistol, "Understood."

It was a wonder Amelia did not realize 3T liked her.

"Wonderful," the captain said as she stepped back. "The two of you need to first go buy some clothes. Be on the lookout for any interesting robot parts to go with the ones we have. You two will also need to buy a D-MES and every training course that you can for it.[24] Moreover, I would also like you to get some kind of entertainment for the living quarters and at least one item of your choice that you think will benefit the crew."

"No problem, Captain," Jason stated as she finished talking. "What are you getting?"

"I plan on getting the things on Mister Larriott's list, clothes for myself as well, and anything else that I think we need or might want. Oh, and training weapons so you two can learn to use your laser blades and firearms."

"Why can't we get clothes together?" 3T asked, wanting to spend time with Amelia.

"I plan on spending a very long time looking at clothes and at many different shops. I doubt you two will want to stay that long, and it will improve productivity as we shop if we split up."

The boys nodded as the group agreed to meet back together at the ship by 2300 HET[25]. They waved to Amelia as they went their separate ways to find some new clothes. It was not missed to Jason, the look on 3T's face. The older boy clearly wanted to go with Amelia.

"So, you like her?" Jay asked.

"You don't? She is a bit uptight, but she is also really cool. She had us steal a spaceship, she knocked out a full grown man in one kick, she has that mysterious thing going, and she is just so confident in herself."

"Hmm, you aren't wrong, maybe not as confident as she pretends to be, but I feel like she just isn't my type. Something is telling me that I shouldn't like her like that, anyway. I'm still trying to figure out her motivations, but she seems like she wants to be a good person."

"Yeah, I guess. She did bring us along with her. I'll try to get to know her, though. She just made a good first impression, you know?"

"You mean a good first impression in offering to give you the chance to go to space and make some money or the fact that she is a girl that talked to you."

3T blushed as he replied, "Bit of both, I guess."

Jason laughed and then pointed to a sign, "That looks like a sign for a clothes store. Let's go in."

The two boys entered the store and were immediately taken aback at the large selection of clothes. There were mannequins that had suits for very fancy parties. There were shelves full of robes made of all different kinds of materials. There was a place, in the back, that had several hundred different pairs of shoes. They saw pants and shirts of all kinds all over the store.

A very snobbish looking old man strolled over to the boys and said, with much enthusiasm, "Welcome to Valda's Vestments, gentlemen. I am Valda! Clothing extraordinaire! How may I be of service today?"

"Hi, Mister Valda. I'm 3T and this is my friend Jason. We just got a sign-on bonus from our ship captain and we were told to buy clothes."

"Say no more, Mister 3T! I, Valda, have you covered!"

Valda pulled out a measuring tape and immediately started sizing up the boys. Neither of them had ever been sized for anything before. Even still, they stood still as Valda measured them.

"One question before we start in earnest. Where is your ship heading, Mister Jason?"

"A bit of everywhere, I think. Our captain plans on going on an adventure," Jason replied as Valda finished measuring.

"Bit of everywhere, eh? Alright. I have things for that. First, though," Valda said as he quickly fetched several different articles of clothes, "Free trade. Your clothes are awful. I have outfits that match nearly exactly. No charge, just go to the changing room and put them on. Looking like homeless bums is no way to start a space adventure."

The two boys looked at each other, surprised, as Valda handed them outfits that were, indeed, almost just like their own tattered clothes. The boys shrugged as they proceeded to go get changed.

"Don't forget to get all of your belongings out of your pockets," Valda yelled as the boys changed and he flew all around the store gathering materials.

The clothes fit the boys better than anything they had ever worn before. The jackets were much better quality than the ones they had taken off. The boys were shocked at how good the other looked when they emerged from the dressing rooms. However, Valda greeted them as they exited before they could say a word to each other.

"Looking great, boys! Alright, I went and fetched you each five pairs of shorts, five pairs of varying pants, two suits depending on if it is a formal event or a date, six robes in styles of varying human and alien cultures, ten shirts for many different occasions, another jacket each beside the ones I gave you, a pair of everyday shoes to replace the crude you have on your feet already, a pair of Ultorian style boots that will automatically attach to metal if gravity is lost, a pair of dress shoes to go with the suits, a set of swimming shorts, and all of the undergarments you could ever need, except wool socks. I am out of wool socks. All top name clothing lines and reinforced with a fiber that will never show any wear and tear."

Jay and 3T were shocked at all of the things Valda had gathered in the short span of them changing clothes. It was Jason that spoke first.

"How much?"

"400, each."

"3T?"

"I think that is going to be fair. The time it took Valda is worth that."

"I guess you have a deal," Jason said, as he and 3T pulled out their UC cards to pay.

"Thank you, gentlemen," Valda said as he accepted the payment.

The quick clothes shop owner pulled out two bags from behind his counter that seemed like normal backpacks.

"These are on the house, my young friends. They're Void Bags.[26] They hold about ten times what they look like they will. In volume, not weight. Don't stick any heavy objects in them. They will pop," Valda announced as he packed each boys' clothes into seperate bags, a black one for 3T and a white one for Jason.

The fact the colors matched their Exclon uniforms underneath their clothes was not lost on them. They moved to collect their new bags, none-the-less, as they were not going to decline something as mind boggling as a bag that was bigger on the inside than the out. As 3T took his first, he could not help but to speak.

"Thank you, Mister Valda. I have just started traveling the galaxy, but you might be the best person at their job out there and, by far, the most generous"

"Thank you, young sir. Feel free to compliment me all you wish."

As Jay took his bag he had to ask, "Why are you giving us these, sir?"

"I had a dream when I was young, too. I dreamed of going on an adventure to these alien worlds and introducing them to Earthling fashion. I couldn't leave my dear, sweet mother, though. So, here I am. Selling clothes and supporting would-be spacefarers. Just let the aliens know where you got your style."

Jason nodded as the shop keeper finished his explanation. The shopkeeper smiled at the boys but then insisted on getting back to work as another customer entered his shop. The boys waved goodbye as Valda started his routine on a new client. The boys were very satisfied at how quick the trip to get clothes was.

"What now, 3T? Robot parts?"

"Might as well, I guess."

The boys mainly talked about the new outfits they were wearing as they walked. They agreed they were both looking much better. They laughed when 3T said no one could even tell they were homeless street urchins just the previous day. They ended up walking quite a ways in their search for robot parts. They each had to stop a few times to buy random items that they passed by in that market town. Jason was the first to stop to get a new trinket. There was a crystal that had an image of Mars on the inside. This crystal floated just a little ways off of the table, and nothing the boys did to it made it drop. The shopkeep, a Folmosclonistarian, insisted that the crystal was magic, but the boys thought it was an issue with the language barrier.[27] They really did need those translator chips. Jay ended up buying the crystal for only 5 UC and stuck it in his bag.

3T was not much better at staying on task. He insisted they stop to get some genuine leather belts at one shop and ended up spending 20 UC on 10 belts. He then had to stop to get a small hand mirror that could show the user their bones and muscles. The mirror was of course a scam, and it merely used cameras to apply a filter to make the user look like their muscles or skeleton. That set him back nearly 80 UC. However, he also made Jason stop when they noticed two merchants bickering over trying to get a locked crate open.

"I think I can open that crate," 3T said, interrupting the bickering merchants.

"You? You're just a kid!" The uglier of the two merchants jeered.

"How about we bet on it then?" Jason said as 3T shrugged and started to walk away.

"You want to wager on your pal, eh? How about 100 UC if he can't open it and he can keep the contents if it opens?" The other merchant suggested and the uglier nodded in agreement, too.

"Deal. 3T, do your thing."

3T spun back around and pulled out his handy laser knife that he had already picked two locks with on that adventure and proceeded to do it again. The merchants were displeased that they had lost the bet, but they cheered up that the contents of the crate were just a box filled with ten bracelets labeled in an alien language. The merchants explained how they thought it would have been salt, as that was their business. The salt merchants were grateful when 3T explained how the laser blade pushed the pins into place and how the metal rod that the laser protruded from was then able to twist the lock into place. Still, the boys took the small box of alien bracelets

"Definitely salt thieves," Jason said as they parted with the merchants.

"I agree. Good thing it wasn't salt. Those idiots would probably just attack us and take it back if it was."

"Probably. I shouldn't have made the bet."

"It's fine. We made out with the goods. What were we looking for again?" 3T asked, forgetting what they needed next.

"Robot parts."

"Right, I thought it was magic crystals."

"I was starting to think it was belts and jewelry," Jason replied with just as much sass.

"Say what you will, but those are some very nice belts."

"Sure. Hey, look!"

Jay had spotted a sign up ahead that simply said "D-MES's" and was now pointing it out to 3T.

"Right," 3T muttered. "Amelia ordered us to pick up one and to get plenty of courses installed."

The two boys hurried to the store but entered it slowly. Neither one of them happened to like the D-MES due to what happened after they each finished their basic education training on them. Back in their alley on Earth, Jay and 3T discussed how they each had finished the courses and were, therefore, considered 'fully educated' by the Earth's government. For Jason, that meant he had to go work in the salt mine when he finished at age 11. For 3T it meant he was ready to leave his home to set off on an adventure when he finally finished only a couple of months back. He missed his brothers and parents.

The shopkeeper of the D-MES shop greeted them as they entered. This time instead of an old, odd man, they found that the shop was run by a robot.[28]

"Welcome. I am designated as SKA01129701.[29] Please state your educational goals," The robot stated in a cold, robotic voice, almost immediately as the two friends entered.

"Um, hi. Yes, we need an D-MES and every educational course relevant to being a space farer," Jason stated as 3T started to look around.

"Programs related to 'SPACE FARING' includes mechanics, engineering, medical practice, close range combat, long range combat, robotics, alien history, alien diplomacy, normal magic, cooking, wilderness survival, path finding, whittling, knot-tying, filmography, piloting, physics, black magic, leadership, commerce, psychology, sociology, philosophy, space faring, ship construction, battle magic, creative writing, janitorial duties, geography, and basic education," The robotic shopkeeper rattled off in a very broken, yet very fast, pace.

"Did it just say black magic?" 3T asked as he stopped looking aimlessly to listen to the list.

"And normal magic. How do you learn magic from a training course?" Jay replied.

"You don't. Magic isn't real. Like werewolves."

"What is your deal with werewolves? Either way, we'll see. Alright, SKA-701, how much for the system and the courses?" Jay asked.

"The D-MES and all courses related to 'SPACE FARING' will come to a total of 1,100 Ultorian Credits or 1,182,796 Earth Credits," The SKA unit said in its electronic voice.

3T nearly fell over when he heard the amount of Earth Credits.

"Holy crude," 3T said. "I had no idea that was that many credits."

"Yeah, it is a lot. We need to pool our money. How about 550 UC each?"

"Sounds good," 3T stuttered out as he pulled out his UC card to transfer the credits to Jay.

Jason transferred the 1,100 UC to the SKA bot, and the robot started to download the many courses into the D-MES helmet. The download took nearly an hour, in which the boys ended up playing a game where they flicked the floating Mars crystal that Jason had bought earlier at each other. Eventually, the boys were able to collect the D-MES and stick it in the younger boy's bag. Jay remarked on only having 545.5 UC left. 3T sighed when he noticed he only had 450. The boys left, not thinking to thank the robot shop keeper.

"Alright, all we need is to get some robot parts and find something useful for the crew," Jay said. He was drained from having to move through the crowded streets and having to interact with so many new people.

"Right," 3T replied. "There's a robotic store over there."

3T led them a little ways down the crowded street where they ducked into a rather large robotics store. The store had all kinds of broken machines. Arms, legs, treads, bodies, heads, and parts that the boys could not guess their purposes were all over the place. There were no other customers in the store as the boys entered, which was odd for such a large store. The two teens knew why almost immediately, though. The shopkeeper stood to greet them. The young men thought about running, but they froze as the alien approached.

Before them stood the largest Ultorian they had ever seen, standing nearly 8ft tall and having to stoop to not hit his head on the ceiling and spanning nearly 6ft across. If that was not horrifying enough, the lizard features of the Ultorian race showed fiercely on his face as he bared his dinosaur-like teeth at them. The thick mane around his head only increased his fierce look. All six eyes were black as night. The most terrible feature, however, was the fact his arms were replaced with that of the robots that surrounded them.

"Welcome, hu-mans," The lizard-lion-robot man squeaked out in a very comedical, high pitch voice.

The boys had no choice but to chuckle, despite how terrifying the monster of an alien was before them.

"That can't be your real voice," Jay said, trying to hide his laughter.

"Of course not," came the alien's reply with a very gruff voice in a very clear common Earth language. "I just like to have a little fun. Not many stay long enough to hear the voice change. Welcome to Azion's Robotics."

"That's wonderful, honestly, sir. Are you Azion?" Jay asked.

"Aye, I am. What can I do you for?"

"We have a busted robot on our ship and our captain asked us to get interesting parts for it."

"I think I have you covered. How much are you looking to spend?"

"I have about 400 UC to spend. What about you, 3T?

3T was looking out the window when Jay asked him this question. He hardly reacted to the question at first.

"Uh, Jay, I think my UC card has a problem. I'm going to quickly pop out to the nearest UC machine to get it examined."

Jay looked at his friend for a moment before replying, "That's fine. I'll be here."

"Great," 3T blurted as he rushed out of Azion's store.

"What's up with him?" Azion asked.

"I'm not sure yet," Jay mumbled before turning back towards the alien shopkeeper.

"Well, kid, I think I have a pretty good deal for you. I have 3 bots worth of outdated, refurbished parts in a crate in the back. 300 UC for that. Pick out a few other bits to make up the other 100 from the selection around you."

"That sounds like a plan, I guess," Jason stated while still thinking about 3T.

It wasn't hard for Jay to find 100 UC worth of interesting parts around him. He managed to find two hand attachments that could transform into dozens of different tools, including drills, hammers, and a welding torch for 25UC a piece. He also pulled an eye attachment that would allow the robot to switch between several different types of vision like thermal, infrared, night, and threat evaluation. That piece was only 20 UC. The 30 UC left that he had intended to spend went to a special paint that could be mixed into any color and provide the robot protection to up to E-Class lasers. These buys left Jay with only 145.5 UC to spend on something useful to the crew.

Azion was very happy to show the boy all of the parts in the crate that he had mentioned as well. The crate had hundreds of different things. It was like the shop was shrunk down and put inside the box. After examining all of the spare limbs, joints, wires, and circuit boards, Jason was convinced of its value. The two talked over the details of the purchase as Jason transferred Azion the credits he owed.

"Well, boy, it has been great doing business. The crate will be delivered to your ship. Dock 0005, you said? Can I help you with anything else while you wait on your friend?"

"Yes, actually, Azion. I need to get something useful for the crew. Do you have any ideas?"

"Hmm… I do have an idea."

"That isn't more robot parts?"

The pair chuckled together before Azion went on, "No, no, nothing of the sort. You should get a World Atlas! They are little globes that record the planets they go on and can give you detailed reports on any planet's geography that it touches. Based on an old technology that some people think is magic. Only a few, 100, True Atlases exist. However, the knock-offs are about 100 UC and are still really good. They don't last forever, though. Not like the real ones."

"Where can I get one of those?" Jay asked with intrigue.

"There is a shop, Bert's Geography Supplies, right down the street. Go on, I'll tell your pal where you went."

"Sounds like a good break," Jay said, hopping to his feet.

Azion pointed him in the right direction and the youngest crewmate on that unnamed ship sprang off in that direction. It was at this point that the good fortune that had swarmed over Jason would disappear. The boy was being followed by several horrible individuals. Jay almost made it to the store with the World Atlases, but as he passed a particularly dark alleyway, he was pulled away

from his destination, never to make it there.

Chapter 8: Red Dusters

Jason was not prepared for the two brutes that sprang out from the alley. They were on him before he knew what was happening. The other pedestrians that were in the street merely looked away or hurried off. As one grabbed him around the body, pinning his arms to his side, the other man covered his mouth to muffle his yells for help. Jay was beyond terrified as he was drugged into that alley that was as dark as the abyss. The boy kicked and struggled with all of his might, but a thin 13 year old kid that had consisted of only dumpster scraps for six months was no match for two fully grown, burley thugs.

He struggled as the thugs pulled him to the end of the alley, and he kicked like a kangaroo as he was pulled into a backside alley. Now, away from the street, where Jason had little chance to be saved by someone else, the boy was tossed to the ground. Looking up from the Martian dirt, Jay noticed the alley he had been drugged to had even more horrendous thugs in it. Counting the two that drug him there that now blocked his exit, there were six goons surrounding the kid. All of them wore a leather jacket as red as the dirt.

"What do you people want?" Jay said with panic in his voice as he sat up on his knees.

"*What do we want,*" One of the thugs, a woman who looked to be in her early 20's and had scars over her eyes, mocked. "We just want what you've got."

"Yeah, rat," Said a gruff voice behind Jay coming from a large man with a very round belly and head.

"So, we are just going to take it," A hissing voice sneered from a man that had a nose like that of a snake's.

The large man with the round head ripped the white Void Bag off of the boy's shoulders and handed it to the other large man, this one having a beard that reached his stomach, that was beside him.

"Yes," Came a monotone voice from the long bearded man. "This chump has tons of very expensive clothes in here."

"Just take them," Jay pleaded in fear of the vicious group that had surrounded him.

"Oh, and what's this?" The monotone voice continued without acknowledging the scared boy. "A D-MES? Oh, yes, we hit the jackpot with this little one."

Jason looked shocked as he heard those words, 'A D-MES'. He could easily let them take his clothes. He did not need them. He only had two pairs of clothes the entire time he lived in his own alley back on Earth and only three when he was with his foster family. However, the D-MES was not his. It belonged to Amelia, his new friend, his captain. She had given him a bed. Food. A laser blade. Hundreds of UC. How would she act if he let her down so soon? Would he be kicked off the ship for being such a failure? These thoughts all crossed the poor lad's mind.

"Wait? The D-MES isn't mine. You can't have that," Jay stated with a shaky voice, not wanting to let the crew down on the first day.

The whole group laughed at Jason's attempt to stand up to them.

"Don't you know who we are? You came to Blackfire and didn't know who we are?" The scar-eyed lady said as if she was offended.

"We are the Red Dusters![30] We run this town," The hissing voice chimed in.

One of the other two thugs in the alley, this one looking young, no older than 17, that had not yet said anything, spoke up next, "We take what we want!"

"Yeah, kid," The other thug, who was identical to the last one to speak, chimed in, though with a slightly more feminine voice. They both had such wolfish grins.

The scar-eyed lady punched Jay on the side of his head, knocking the boy back down in the dirt.

"Yeah, and after we take everything you have, and after you give us every credit you have left, we are going to find that friend you were with and do the same to him. Ah, you seem surprised. Oh, we have been watching you since our lookout said that a very fancy ship landed at our dock and only three kids got out. Speaking of which, we also will find that girl, too," The hissing man with the snake nose said as menacing as possible.

One of the larger men, the round headed one, kicked Jay in the stomach as the kid tried to get up. Jason was already pretty beat up from the struggle he put up resisting being pulled into the alley. He was hurting.

"You can't," Jason coughed as he tried to get a breath. "You can't mess with my friends."

That gang did not like being told what they could or could not do. The hissing man punched straight down on the back of

Jay's head, nearly making him black out. The scar-eyed woman stomped down on the boy's hand, breaking two bones in it. The bearded man kicked Jason right in the face, eschewing the teen's nose.

Jay was used to being abused. His foster parents had swung at him on a frequent basis. Their blows could not compare to the blows of these thugs, though. Jason was hurt, bad. He was barely conscious at that point. Blood dripped from his broken nose. What could he do? He rolled over and could not resist as one of the twin Red Dusters pulled his UC card from his pocket and forced his hand to approve a transfer. The other twin smiled as he watched his card glow green. Jason was now broke.

The one twin replaced the card into Jay's pocket and turned to his mates, "We are done here. Let's find the other two."

The gang laughed in agreement as they started to leave the alley. The last to leave, the one with the monotone voice, carried the white backpack in his left hand. Jay watched the bag sway before the man disappeared around the corner. Jason cried into the dirt, but he made up his mind.

He could not leave that bag. Amelia trusted him, and Jason did not want to be proven right that he would fail the crew. The boy raised to his feet. He could hardly stand at first. His legs were shaking. He had to act though.

Jason started off, at first, slow, but it was only a moment before he was sprinting, faster than he had ever ran before, after the Red Dusters.

The bearded man with the bag was just leaving the alley into the main street when Jay rounded the corner. The boy was determined. He caught up with the monster of a man before the bearded thug could turn around. Jason grabbed the Void Bag and managed to snatch it from the loose grip of the man. The boy did not stop running.

By the time that the rest of the Red Dusters knew what had happened, Jay had managed to run past the group, bag in hand. He had nearly ten paces on the thugs and a running start before the man with the hissing voice yelled to get that child and end him! The group took off after him, and they began to gain ground. The twins split off into an alley so they would be able to prevent an escape down a side street by the boy. The scar-eyed lady and the hissing man were gaining ground quicker than the rest. The round head man and the bearded guy were just too big to keep up as they hardly ever ran.

Jason knew he was not the fastest runner, however. They would catch him. So, he had to get to safety! Where could he go, though? He had barely been in this town half a day. He had barely been on that planet for half a day! He did not have to go far before he saw his only hope: Azion's Robotics! There was no way the monster of a person, Azion, would ever let someone cause trouble in his shop. He was actually very sweet and who would mess with an individual that was a giant Ultorian cyborg.

The shop was right there! Jay had a good five paces on his pursuers. He was going to make it! Jason slid to a stop at the door and grabbed the handle! He jerked at it with everything his broken body had left!

It did not open. The door was locked.

Jason only had time to let one sigh escape. One sigh that contained all hope the teen had left. The scar-eyed woman grabbed the boy and slung him to the ground. Jay went sliding and rolling away down the dirt walkway towards the rest of the Red Dusters. The four thugs quickly surrounded him and began to kick and stomp at him. It was over. Jason would meet his end under that green-ish, butterscotch sky.

At least he would have. Jay heard a sound that he recognized. A clear 'PHEWF!' The sound that a laser gun makes. He heard one shot, and the kicking stopped. He heard a second shot and the biggest guy, the one with the round head, was knocked to the ground! A third shot! The group of Red Dusters

dived into cover behind crates and dumpsters and into alleys as the

shots flew at them.

Jay looked in the direction of his savior, one eye swollen

shut, as the gang hid and started to pull out their own blasters.

There, a few buildings down, stood 3T, laser pistol in hand. He

was not holding his aim steady. The street cleared out as the gang

started to return fire! 3T had to run forward and dive behind a crate

himself to avoid being hit. Jason, still clutching his white bag, was

still too far away to pull into cover with him. Jay was still

conscious, though. He started crawling towards his friend.

The gang did not notice the youngest boy start to crawl

away. They had a fire fight to win! The three that were still

standing had not stopped firing from cover since they pulled out

their own weapons. They were not very skilled with firearms,

though, and the guns they used were rather crumby. They missed

hitting 3T with every shot! The 15 year old was getting lucky as one beam of pure energy zipped past his head and another blasted a decent burn onto the wall beside him.

Jay was in a terrible state. He was clawing his way to 3T with one arm while he clutched the white bag in the other. His ribs were hurting, maybe even broke, and he could hardly get air. His nose was pouring even more blood now than it had in the alley. Dirt and blood filled his mouth, and his head was throbbing. Jay needed help.

"Stay there, Jay!" 3T yelled as another laser crashed into his cover. "You'll be okay! I'm coming, buddy!"

"3... T... Run," Jay squeaked out through the blood, worried that he was going to get his best friend killed.

He could see his friend shooting blindly from cover. Every shot the teen took at his enemies, three fired back at him. It seemed to be a stalemate, though. Timolas Thomas Tymes had used a gun several times before back home on the farm. He had learned to hunt to protect the dairy herd from predators while they grazed.

However, he had never killed anything before, just shot at it to scare it off. This time, the predators did not run. Worse still, they had lasers of their own.

The stalemate was eventually broken, though. The large, round headed man, who 3T had shot in the shoulder, rose to his feet. 3T's F-Class pistol would only kill with multiple shots and that man was too big for an F-Class laser to stun for long. The gang saw their comrade get up, and they all realized that that laser pistol would only hurt and not kill. They could rush the kid who ambushed them.

"He has a little laser. Get him!" One of them yelled.

3T had hit the other big guy, the one with the beard, as they rushed towards him. He went down, but not long enough to matter. Moreover, the scar-eyed lady and the hissing man were too quick. They had made it to 3T and tossed him from his cover. He barrel rolled from the throw, and ultimately, he landed on his feet. It did not matter though. He was surrounded. Four to one.

3T held his laser blaster up and spun around, pointing wildly at his opponents, trying to make them stay back.

"Well," The hissing man started. "You saved us some trouble. However, since you attacked us, we will not be as kind to you as we were your little friend."

The gang laughed as they started to circle, spinning around 3T. The round headed one made sure to step on Jason as he went. They all raised their blasters in unison, ready to finish off Timolas Thomas Tymes.

Before the first trigger was pulled though, there was a gasp as the round headed man toppled in half. As his torso fell to the ground, and his legs soon followed, the other three Red Dusters were greeted by a site that, if they knew better, would chill them down to their souls. To 3T and Jay, who was still lying down upon the ground, it was a sight of hope. There stood a black clad figure with a flowing charcoal cloak. Her eyes were glowing red, or maybe that was just an illusion from the pulsing red and purple katana that she held in her hands.

"Get Jay back to the ship, 3T," Amelia said with violent anger in her voice.

"But Cap…"

"Now!"

3T did not try to argue anymore. He rushed to scoop Jason up to help carry him back to the ship. The scar-eyed lady did not want to allow that, especially, after seeing her friend be split in two. She pointed her pistol back at 3T's head. As she was about to fire, however, her gun was sundered in two!

Amelia had saved 3T from that gangster, once again! The rest of the gang, the guy with the beard and the hissing man, aimed for Amelia. They could not possibly miss that close to her.

However, they did.

Amelia had somehow dodged a laser blast. That should have been impossible for a human! However, every shot that the duo of gang members fired at Amelia looked as if she was sidestepping. She walked towards them, blade flashing a blood red color. It did not matter how close she got, they could not hit her. The hissing man pushed the scar-eyed woman, who was now weaponless and, therefore, useless to him, at Amelia to slow her down. She was unarmed. So, Amelia spared her. The captain's blade only separated the woman's right arm from her chest. The sword's heat cauterized the wound just a bit as it cut, preventing the scar-eyed lady from bleeding out.

The hissing man was sure that distraction was enough. It was. His laser pistol met its mark. Amelia did not even react to the blast hitting her stomach and scorching through her clothes.

The hissing man had to run. He shoved his last comrade forward.

"Get this devil! She is a third your size, Naldo!"

"Hmm... Naldo. First person I will have to kill with a name."

Naldo did not have enough time to do more than take one swing at Amelia. The hissing man was already sprinting full speed away by the time that Naldo, the bearded man with the monotone voice toppled over, split in half like the bald man. The last gang member picked the wrong way to go, though. The way he went was the same as how the boys went to get back to their ship at Dock 0005. This forced Amelia to be in hot pursuit, whether she intended to let him run away or not.[31]

The hissing man knew it was going to be all over when he noticed Amelia pursuing him. End of the line. However, he saw the two boys running ahead of him, Jay barely standing, holding on to 3T's neck. The last gang member was not to die and leave this devil girl feeling like she had won. He stopped and aimed at the back of the wounded boy.

PHEWF

The injured child had fallen. His friend barely held his friend's head up out of the dirt. The hissing man aimed once more at the other boy. This time it would be a headshot. The hissing man, satisfied with the chaos he was creating, even smiled as he saw hope not to be sliced in two halves by the dark phantom quickly approaching him from behind. The twins, the two Red Dusters who had taken the back alleys earlier when chasing Jay, appeared ahead of the boys with their pistols already drawn.

He watched as the twins pointed their laser pistols up at the demon behind him. So, the hissing man thought. It was over. How could even the devil dodge two lasers at once? The twins were always in perfect sync and never missed. The hissing man smiled wide in the moment as these truths appeared in his mind. It was unfortunate that a man so horrible would die with a smile on his face. The twins' shots did hit their mark. One blast to the right eye, and one to the left. That was how the hissing man died. Alone and betrayed.

Chapter 9: Surviving

After 3T saw his would-be killer fall onto his back, he looked at his saviors. As he looked up, he first saw the jackets. More Red Dusters. Then he saw their faces!

"Zeb! Zed!"

"Hey," 3T's older brother and sister said in unison.

"What are you doing here? And in a gang!?"

"No time for that," Zed, 3T's sister, started. "We need to get him help."

Amelia was approaching the group as Zed said that. She still had that anger in her glowing red eyes. She casually lobbed off the hissing man's head as she passed by him. Though, he was already dead. She was annoyed that she did not get to pay him back for what he had done to her friends. 3T saw her coming and could tell she was coming for the twins.

"Wait! These two are my siblings!"

Amelia stopped and stared at the twins and 3T.

"Get Jay to the ship. Medical Bay. Now!"

3T signaled his twins to help him carry the now unconscious Jason, who was still clutching his bag. Amelia watched on. She was still in a rage. Her temper had gotten the best of her. She breathed in deeply. It took several breaths before the captain was able to turn her blade off. It glowed a moment longer after she had turned it off. Her eyes glowed red for several moments longer still.

Amelia hurried off after her crew. She was truly afraid she would lose the first friends she had ever made on the first day.

Amelia had just caught up as the Tymes siblings reached the space ship. They were all greeted by a surprising sight. A massive creature of a person was moving down the ramp out of their ship! Amelia immediately started to reach for her sword again. However, she stopped as 3T yelled out to the monster.

"Azion! Help! Jay has been shot!"

"Huh?"

Azion only looked up and looked at the scene for a minute before springing into action. He ran over to the kids, faster than any human could move, but he was no human. Azion lifted the unconscious boy up into his mighty robotic arms and turned back to the ship.

Azion did not even ask for directions as he burst onto the ship as if he knew the way. The Ultorian had burst up the two flights of stairs before the Tymes children and Amelia had even made it onto the ship. Azion went straight to the Med Bay and gently laid the boy he had ushered out of his shop, less than half an hour earlier, onto the examination table. The beast of an alien was already getting medical supplies for treatments out from various containers as the table scanned the boy for injuries, and the captain appeared at the door with the Tymes's right behind her.

"What happened?" Lariott asked in a panic as he pushed past the group at the door to help Azion.

"He was attacked by some goons!" 3T exclaimed in panic.

"Then he was shot by one of them," Amelia rasped out as if she was out of breath.

"Goons? Hmm… Like those two?" Azion asked while filling a needle with some kind of gel.

"No, they weren't with the others," 3T said before the twins could speak.

"Actually, we were with them," Zeb started.

"And we helped steal his money, and the others beat him," Zed finished.

As Zed finished, Amelia had already landed a solid kick to Zeb's chest.

"You did this!" She yelled as that glow flickered in her eyes again.

The twins both looked down as if to say yes and that they deserved what Amelia would do to them.

Before Amelia could draw her laser katana, 3T stepped in front of the twins to stop her.

"Wait, Captain. These two are my family! Please don't…"

3T couldn't finish before Amelia cut him off, "Captain!? Captain!? You call me that now! I told you! I TOLD you that Jason was not to be left alone in this town because of filth like your 'family' here! They beat him to where he couldn't move! They shot him! AND you let it happen! This is your fault as much as it is these two sacks of…"

"Captain," Came a weak voice from the Med Bay behind them. "It wasn't his fault."

Jay was hardly able to move, but he regained consciousness right as Amelia started in on 3T.

"Captain," Jay said, trying to regain some air. "It was my fault, I failed the crew. I told 3T I would stay…"

Amelia pushed into the room and quickly took Jay's hand, "No, Jay. It wasn't your fault. You are not to blame for being attacked."

3T came and put his hand on Jay's shoulder, tears in his eyes, "You will never fail us, Jay. Amelia is right, it was my fault. I didn't have to leave you alone."

"I shouldn't have split from you either. We could have all stayed together in a group. I knew it was dangerous, and I made a bad call because I am selfish," Amelia exclaimed as tears now rolled down her cheeks.

Jay only frowned. He could not help but to blame himself. He made a mistake and it nearly got everyone hurt or killed. Jason was now in tears from his own thoughts. Amelia assumed they were from the pain, but Larriott and Azion had already given him a high quality pain killer in a shot, as well as one that would start healing his broken bones. That would take a few days though. 3T knew Jay well enough to know that the tears were from something else, but he was not sure what.

"He needs rest," Azion spoke up, breaking the silence that started to feel the room. "Other than that he is fine. A few broken bones. Easy fix. Based on the scans, that Exclon suit he has on under his clothes stopped any serious laser damage. Though, it did feel like a very hard punch, I bet."

"I wouldn't know," Jay rasped in reply. "I was out as soon as it hit."

Azion gave a terrible smile with his fanged teeth.

"Thank you, Mister Azion," Amelia said as she let go of Jay's hand. "How much do I owe for your help?"

"It's on the house. I like this kid, and he already bought a lot of parts from me."

"Is that why you were on the ship?" 3T asked.

"Yes, I came and delivered them. Your pilot then paid me to load it and the other four crates that had already been delivered.

"Well, thank you, Mister Azion."

"Just make sure the kid gets plenty of rest. Bed rest for three days and no work for at least two weeks," Azion said knowing that Jay would be as good as new in less than a week. "I have to get back to my shop."

Azion patted Jason's arm and turned to leave. He was almost in the stairwell before 3T and Amelia both yelled and waved goodbye to him. Larriott was still fiddling in the Med Bay, making sure all of Azion's scans were right, which they were. The twins spoke at this point.

"We should go, too," One said.

"We are truly sorry," Said the other before they started to leave.

"Wait!" Amelia said in anger as she remembered they were there. "You need to be punished for doing this to my friend."

3T looked like he was about to step in when Jason spoke again.

"They never touched me, Amelia. Just robbed me."

"They saved my life, as well," 3T added.

Amelia thought for a second while staring holes through Zeb and Zed. She saw the patchy clothes they had on under their Mars red jackets. They looked hungry, too. Crime does not pay, or so, Amelia imagined.

"In light of what my crew and friends stated, I have only one option."

Amelia continued to stare down the twins. The twins were terrified of her verdict, but they accepted that they deserved whatever it was.

"Forced conscription."

"What?!" Everyone in the room including the distracted Larriott and the injured Jay exclaimed together.

"Yes. You will work on this crew until you repay Jason for all of his injuries. You will be provided uniforms, food, water, a place to sleep, and shelter. You, being clearly very good shots, shall be our turret operators in battle. Beyond combat, you will be expected to help with all chores and maintenance of the ship. You will only be paid a small allowance until Jason's injuries are repaid. Understood?"

At the exact same time, both Zeb and Zed pulled off their red jackets, threw them down on the floor, and stomped on them.

"Understood, Captain!"

3T was extremely grateful for what the captain just did for his siblings. Jay smiled as he knew what family meant to Timolas. Amelia simply replied by ordering them to go secure the cargo and insure the other crates were loaded by Azion or if more had arrived after he had finished.

Larriott, Amelia, and 3T all helped Jason to his bedroom. Larriott assured everyone that Jay would be okay and agreed he did not need to do chores for two weeks, knowing the same information Azion did. 3T sat the white Void Bag of Jay's down by his bed. It was amazing the boy had not dropped it during the whole fight. 3T and his siblings prepared dinner as Amelia sat with Jason. The injured boy refused to eat, having his friends just leave a plate by his bed.

Jason insisted that he really just wanted to sleep. Amelia agreed to leave him in his privacy. Though, she did worry about his injuries. She was kinda glad to leave, though. Especially since the blast she took from the hissing man's pistol had actually cracked one of her ribs, too, and she was in a bit of pain herself. Before leaving, Amelia confirmed to Jay that they would be leaving Mars immediately. She thought it was unwise to kill a few people and leave another in a critical state and stay in town. Especially if they had a gang that would try to get revenge.

Jason was still awake fifteen minutes later as the ship started to take off. The artificial gravity stayed on in his room, so he only noticed the lift off as the planet started to disappear from the window in his room.

Jay did not want to sleep as they started to fly back off into space. He wanted to cry. He wanted to think of himself as less of a failure, but he could not. These thoughts still plagued him as he finally drifted off. Jason was the only one on the crew that slept that night, or even the next, as the Tymes children and Amelia all blamed themselves for what happened even more than he did.

Chapter 10: Trying to Stay Calm

It was a terrible next few days for the crew of that unnamed vessel. Jason could hardly sleep, despite being ordered to stay in bed by both Amelia and Larriott. The boy had too much on his mind. The first day, Jay could only think about what happened on Mars. He wondered what he could have done differently. He did not have to let 3T leave the robotics shop without him. He did not have to leave Azion's before 3T got back. He could have just accepted the mugging and not fought to keep his bag. He could have been more vigilant and noticed that the Red Dusters had them marked.

It was during these thoughts that the boy heard a knock on his door.

"Jay, do you need anything?"

It was Amelia. She could not stop worrying about her friend. She knocked on Jay's door nearly every hour. Jason, not wanting to talk to anyone at the time, hardly ever replied. It was only when the captain insisted she come in and deliver him breakfast and dinner that she ever opened the door. Jay pretended to be asleep as she entered at those times, too.

"He barely has eaten anything," Amelia worried as she left the room with the previous meal, hardly touched by Jay.

Amelia was in a terrible mood, herself. The captain blamed herself for not protecting her crew. She was the one that insisted the two homeless boys come with her to space. She thought that meant it was her duty to protect them. Isn't that what a good captain would do?

It did not help that the laser blast she took cracked one of her ribs, and she was in a bit of pain herself. Amelia only knew how to deal with her emotions and pain in one way, though.

"Captain, I feel like this is a bit unfair," 3T protested as his siblings and himself stood across from Amelia holding training swords.

Amelia, having spent a decade of her life training to fight in a dozen different ways, agreed that a three on one fight with training swords was unfair.

"You are right, Mister Timolas. I'll drop my sword and I will only use it if I can tag the crate behind you and then cross back over on this side of the room to get it."

3T was happy that the captain had decided to start using his first name instead of calling him Mister Tymes. When the boy asked Amelia about it, the captain told him that she had only called him mister because, as captain, she wanted to show respect to her crew, but she also did not feel like a very good captain. She also explained that since she 'forced' his older twin siblings to join, there were too many Tymes's on the ship to stick with that system.

"No, Captain," Timolas started, insisting that he call her captain. "I mean, you are good, but it is three to one."

3T picked the wrong word choice. Amelia was too focused to hear what 3T was trying to say and only heard three to one, which sounded to her like 3-2-1.

"Go!" The captain yelled as she burst into action.

Zeb was the first to realize the training had already started. The male twin swung his practice sword, which was a wooden greatsword, at Amelia. The captain easily vaulted over the horizontal slash, but she also, still being angry that the twins helped attack her friends, managed to land a spinning heel kick right on the twin's shoulder. Zed did not like the idea that her twin was about to get destroyed by the captain so she dove forward in a stabbing motion with her matching wood greatsword. Amelia was still in the air. How could she dodge that strike? With ease, apparently.

Amelia had used the spin kick she landed to speed her descent time. Therefore, she was able to land on the ground and duck under Zed's jab. It also gave her enough time to spring forward to grab the female twin by the arm and sling her over her shoulder. 3T saw that this left an opening. He would be able to swing in and land a serious blow with his wood katana. Amelia smiled as she saw the wood blade approaching her midsection.

3T thought his blow would land true around the same time that Amelia would release the judo throw. The captain also thought that, however. So, Amelia dove forward mid throw. This caused her release to spike Zed into the ground instead of tossing her across the workroom.[32] It was when 3T noticed Amelia smiling as his practice sword passed underneath her chest, that he knew that he was next. Amelia landed her dive with a barrel roll, but used the momentum to deliver a leg sweep to 3T before he could try another attack.

By the time the three Tymes siblings had made it back to their feet, Amelia had touched the crate and was ready to fight her way back to her own practice weapon. Their attempts to stop the captain did not go any better the second time. The twins tried to attack together, but Amelia managed to parry both blows and force the twins to smack each other with the practice swords. 3T thought that left him with an opening, again, to deliver a powerful overhead slash. He was stopped by Amelia's hand on his chest.

It seemed to 3T that time had slowed down as Amelia looked into his eyes, their noses only an inch apart. Amelia had a smile that would terrify most people. It was one like a devil would wear. Unsettling. However, Timolas Thomas Tymes thought it was the most beautiful smile in the galaxy. That is why he was unsure if he could not breathe from how close he had been to Amelia or if the blow to his chest momentarily stopped his breathing. He was, however, sure that the way Amelia slammed him shoulder first to the ground from that blow meant that they were never going in slow motion.

The three siblings all managed to get back up, again, but now they saw that Amelia had made it to her practice sword. As if reading each other's minds, all three Tymes kids dropped their weapons and held their hands up in surrender.

While Amelia threw herself into training, which was the thing that brought her any sought of peace, Timolas was busy doing anything to keep from talking with his siblings. He ended up cleaning rooms that had no dirt in them. He arranged and rearranged both his room and the living area multiple times. He organized the workshop after Amelia moved everything around to make room to train.

3T blamed himself as much as Amelia and Jason did. However, he had more confidence in himself than they did. He took on a healthy amount of internalization for the tragedy that struck his friend. He knew he should have stayed with the kid, but

173

he also externalized more and rationalized what would have happened if they did stay together. That gang would have just ambushed 3T, too. They would not have had a chance.

Well, we would have, but only if my siblings decided to help us out, 3T thought to himself. *Why did they attack my friend?*

Chapter 11: Emotions on an Unnamed Star Ship

While Amelia was still feeling down on herself, even after taking out her frustrations in a training session, the three Tymes children were also beating themselves up as well. 3T was beyond happy to see his older twin siblings. Zed and Zeb were the ones that showed him how to pick locks with his laser knife. They were the ones that bought him his first knife. The one he always carried with him. The two of them and 3T with his own twin were always together back on the farm. Even after they were forced off of the farm and the twins left home to find adventure, Timolas Thomas and Thomlas Timothy were the only people in the family to get a letter from them. 3T had to know what made them turn to a life of crime. So, after the first day, he finally confronted them.

"Wait, I thought you two were working real jobs? You said you were on your way to New Pacifica! Why were you in a gang on Mars?" 3T accused his siblings.

"Well, about that," Zeb started.

"We did have work on a ship heading to New Pacifica," Zed continued.

"But we ended up being kicked off the ship,"

"After we ended up realizing the ship was a smuggling vessel,"

"And demanded a larger cut from the venture," Zeb said, finishing the first sentence.

"Of, course. You went along with smuggling. How did you end up in a gang, then?"

"Well, we were sent to the market when we stopped in Blackfire," Zed started this time.

"And the ship we were on, *The Bad Break*, left us there,"[33] Zeb continued.

"We had no money and no job."

"That is when Hillus, the hissing man, found us."

"They tried to mug us like they did your friend,"

"But we were broke."

"A few weeks later, we were officially a part of the Red Dusters."

"They promised to make sure we were provided for and that we could earn hundreds of UC."

"We actually did a terrible job, though."

"Yes, the first credits we actually received were your friends."

"Again, we are sorry for that. We had no idea he was with you," Zed finished.

3T interrupted, with anger in his voice, "You shouldn't have been mugging anyway! What would mom think? You also need to return his credits."

"We know," The twins said together, pitifully.

"I can't believe you two," 3T spat with disdain.

"You'd've done the same!" The twins yelled back.

"No way! I would never be so…"

"So, what?" Zeb asked.

"So, much of a thief?" Zed added.

"Yes!" 3T yelled back.

"What are you talking about?" Zed said incredulously.

"The pilot told us how you stole this ship together," Zeb went on.

"Yeah, this thing is worth millions of UC."

"That is more than every gang of Mars has stolen."

"Combined!" The twins finished together.

"That is different!"

"How?" The twins asked in unison while pushing 3T.

3T, not liking the fact they were right, decided to defend his argument the way only siblings know how.[34] The three of them were in a drag out brawl in the living area when Amelia entered from the kitchen, having just disposed of Jay's breakfast leftovers. She was even angrier now because they had surrendered before she got to use her practice sword, and she really liked to use swords. It did not help that her ribs were hurting even more from that training exercise.

The captain asked no questions before joining the fray. She was easily whopping all three of them since stopping the fight was only a bonus goal for the captain. Especially since they were trying to fight each other still instead of herself. Even the twins had started throwing shots at each other while yelling that it was the other one's idea. It was not going to be a pretty fight. However, the fight came to a stand still much faster than it had started.

Jason, hearing the brawl through his door, decided to check it out. He managed to get up on his feet, though his back was throbbing from the laser blast he had taken. The bones in his hand were already healed, the same as the rest of his broken bones, thanks to the gel Azion and Larriott had injected him with.

However, it still hurt when he picked up the blanket off of his bed to wrap around his shoulders. His breathing was better, but deep breaths still hurt.

No one noticed Jay as he shuffled into the living area. He watched for a minute, but after Amelia sent both Zeb and 3T over the table, he decided that he wanted to sit on the couch. He slowly shuffled to sit down, but he could not help but notice the wrappings on Amelia's midsection as she flipped over Zed as the twin was going to pounce on the downed Zeb. 3T and Amelia had just squared back up when Jason flipped on the entertainment screen to watch some news.[35] All four combatants stopped as that alerted them to the young teen's presence.

"Jay…" 3T started.

"You guys are rather loud," Jason interrupted.

"Yeah, sorry. We just had a disagreement," Zeb inputted.

"We shouldn't have been pushing Tim," Zed finished.

"I threw the first punch, Captain," 3T argued, turning towards the captain.

"That is okay, Mister Timolas. Tensions have been running high all day and yesterday, and it is already nearly 0200." Amelia, still calming down and starting to feel disappointed in not getting to win the fight, replied.

"We should talk about yesterday," Jay interjected before the captain could send everyone to bed.

"Yes, we should pick up first, though," Amelia stated while she looked at the living area that had been trashed during the fight.

"We will get the room cleaned, Captain," The twins blurted out together.

"You should talk with 3T and… Jay, right?" Zeb continued.

"We will also repair the table, if we can." Zed finished.

Amelia sighed and agreed to the twins' idea. She did not really want to talk about the previous day, but she was glad the twins were taking responsibility in fixing the messed up room. The twins rushed off to get some tools to fix some of the broken furniture, and Amelia and 3T sat down on either side of Jason.

"So," 3T started again.

"Thank you," Jason interrupted. "The two of you saved me. I was finished without you both coming to the rescue. You risked your lives to save mine. I've never had anyone that would do that for me."

"You'd have done the same," 3T replied first.

"Nonsense. My life was never at risk," Amelia claimed boldly.

"How did you injure your ribs then?" Jay asked.

"Oh, that. You noticed. I made a mistake. That is all."

"A mistake?" 3T asked. "You?"

"Yes, I failed to dodge one of their laser blasts."

"I thought I was crazy when I looked back and saw you dodge a laser blast. How is that even possible?" 3T asked as if she had done the impossible.

"Well, you cannot dodge laser bolts or beams. Far too fast. However, with cheap laser guns and even some expensive ones, the guns glow a moment before while they build the energy up. Since the blasts are so fast, if you dodge when you see the glow, it looks like you are dodging the beams."

"You're a witch, Amelia," Jay said with astonishment.

"Just a bit. I took a class in battle magic. I never passed it though."

"Battle magic?" 3T asked.

"Yeah. Some of the aliens we humans have met have developed what we would describe as magic. Some Ultorians claim they learned it from a race that they considered gods that went extinct thousands of years ago."

"Oh, we have some courses on magic on our D-MES!" 3T exclaimed. "Do you still have it, Jay?"

"Yeah, it was the reason why I wouldn't give up my bag," Jason said as he instructed 3T to get his bag from his room to show it to Amelia.

"Thank you for not losing the D-MES, Jason, but we could have just bought another."

"You are far too important to risk your life on some dumb schooling device, Jay!"

Amelia and 3T spoke at the same time. Despite trying to make Jason feel better, their words just reinforced to him that he had made a mistake.

"Sorry, it was a mistake," Jason continued as he lowered his head.

"No. You are not to blame, and you did the best anyone in your situation could do. I am extremely proud that you fought to keep the crew's property. Very brave, and it shows I made the right choice in asking you to come with Larriott and myself," Amelia stated without even a hint of dishonesty in her voice. "Speaking of mistakes, though. Why did you leave Jason alone, Mister Timolas?"

"I had an issue with my UC Card, and I had to go get it reset at one of those machines."

"Reset?" Both Amelia and Jason asked together as both had never even heard of such a thing, and they both had had UC Cards for far longer than 3T.

"Yeah," 3T started as his face turned red. "It was having trouble transferring credits."

"It seemed fine when we got clothes and when you gave me the credits for the D-MES," Jay stated as he relaxed on the couch's cushion and held his aching chest.

"Yes, but…"

"Mister Tymes!" Amelia angrily snapped. "Why did you leave Jason alone?"

3T sighed as he looked down at the floor, knowing he could not lie anymore.

"I went to transfer my credits back home to my family," 3T finally let out.

"Transfer your credits back to your family?" Amelia repeated as the twins returned with some brooms and basic repair tools.

"Yeah, I figured they could use a few."

"A few!" The twins blurted in before Amelia or the weary Jason could reply.

"Our parents are barely scraping by!" Zeb started.

"We only ran away from home because they couldn't afford us!" Zed finished.

"Z's, they don't," 3T tried to interject as Amelia and Jason listened to the twins intently.

"Go on, Mister Zed, Miss Zeb," Amelia ordered, cutting 3T off, as the twins paused for a moment to stare at 3T.

"We left home over a year ago due to financial trouble after Antonio De Salina took our family's farm," Zeb continued.

"Tim and Tom agreed that one of them would leave when they finished the basic education course," Zed stated as 3T grew even redder.

"They were to play a game of RPS.[36]"

"Loser had to leave home," Zed finished.

"Had to leave?" Jay asked his best friend.

3T replied with little passion, "Yeah, no one wanted to leave the family behind. I always wanted to go to space, but I would rather have been home, helping our parents make enough money to feed our younger brothers. Someone had to leave, though. There is money to be had in space. I was desperate to get out here to make enough for my family to buy back the farm. It didn't hurt that going to space was also a pipe dream all kids have."

"Same," The twins said in very quiet voices.

Amelia, who had listened to every word without showing any emotions, spoke, "I only have a few thousand UC left after everything I bought on Mars, but I promise, that the three of you will make more than enough money on this crew to buy your family's farm back from that giant piece of shit."

The twins, 3T, and Jay were all taken aback at the determination that Amelia said those words with. She meant those words, and the crew believed that she was going to do whatever she could for them.

Before anyone else could speak, Amelia, who could now see the full picture of the twins' story, continued, "Twins, do not worry about this mess tonight. Clean it in the morning. Go to bed. We will work up a contract tomorrow to help you get paid from the exploits of this ship and its crew."

At first, the twins looked towards Jason as they still owed him for the injuries. Jay nodded his approval of the idea. The twins, who were very tired as they did not sleep the previous night while they thought about how they nearly got their brother killed and the many others they had hurt while in the Red Dusters, agreed to go to sleep this time. They were happy to finally be on track to earn an earnest living.

"Before we go, 3T," Zed started.

"How did you lose to Tom at RPS?" Zeb continued.

"He only ever picked rock."

3T, looking even worse than before, looked his siblings in the eyes.

"I didn't."

No one spoke for a moment as they all realized what 3T's words meant. He was the one who won the right to stay home, but he left so his brother did not have to. The twins only looked away, without saying anything, knowing that 3T sacrificed what they all desired most.

It was a few minutes before anyone said anything after the twins left to go to sleep. The three friends sat quietly on the couch and watched as the news broadcast on the screen before them started playing a weather report from Earth's Neolandia. It was raining there.

"So," Jason broke the silence. "What did you end up buying, Captain?"

"Oh," Amelia started as if she was happy someone asked, glad to be talking about something else. "I first had to get a pair of Pilot Arms for Larriott.[37] He also had me pick up 500 UC worth of Martian Honey. I think he has an addiction to it. He also wanted a specific style of pilot's uniform, like that of his fathers'. I also found a great deal on training weapons. I got, like, two dozen wood swords and a few practice guns. Little A-Class pistols and rifles. Oh, I also got an upgrade circuit for one of our scanners that will allow us to receive job requests that are sent out, like emergencies on other ships or urgent deliveries. I also got a registration device so we can name our ship in an official manner. I had all of that delivered to the ship. I finally went to get myself some clothes. I found this neat little shop called Valda's..."

"That is where we got our clothes," 3T interrupted.

"I hope you tried to negotiate that jerk down. I bought nearly 30 outfits and he tried to charge me 800 UC! The other shop I stopped at after that I got 20 outfits, including this one really cute dress, you'll have to see it later, 3T, for only 500 UC. Anyway, I made Valda lower his price all the way down to 600. He then tried to sell me a Void Bag for 10,000 UC. I got it for only 6,000," Amelia hardly breathed as she told the boys about her day. She did not have anyone that ever cared to listen before.

"I think we paid 400 each at Valda's," Jay mused.

"That is not so bad, boys. What about the Void Bags you were wearing though? Did you steal them? I won't be mad if you did."

The boys laughed for the first time since they separated at the robotics store.

"Of course not," Jason chuckled.

"Valda gave them to us for our adventure. I think he liked the fact we were going to space, and we didn't argue about the price," 3T said through his own chuckles.

Amelia, now very annoyed that she had made such a big financial blunder, decided to change the topic.

"Well, Jason, Timolas, you got the robot parts, clothes, and D-MES, but what about something special for the crew? I know your shopping trip was interrupted."

The boys looked at each other.

"Well," 3T started slowly. "I won these bracelets in a bet."

Jason yawned as 3T ran to his room and returned with his black Void Bag and pulled out the box of bracelets. The captain was stunned at what they were.

"Do you know what those are, Mister Timolas?"

"Bracelets?"

"Those are tele-communication bracelets.[38] Those will allow us to talk to each other from miles away if we are both wearing one on the same frequency. We will not even have to talk out loud."

3T smiled, realizing that he had succeeded in finding something useful. Amelia was even more annoyed that he did not even have to buy them.

"Well, Jason. I know you were attacked. So, do not even worry that you did not get anything," Amelia said in a tone that had a hint at victory in it as she looked over at Jay.

Jay was fast asleep, having dozed off as 3T went to get his bag.

Amelia smiled as Jay's head tilted over.

"Let's get him to bed," Tim suggested.

"Yes, Let us do that."

Amelia and 3T gently woke Jason and helped their still sore friend back to his bed.

The still semi-broken Jay fell right asleep as his friends laid him on his bed. They left him to get some much needed rest.

"Captain?" 3T said as they sat back on the couch.

"Yes, Mister Timolas?"

"Jason did buy one thing."

"What would that be?"

3T went to Jason's bag that was still on the couch from where they showed Amelia the D-MES. He pulled out the ever floating crystal that displayed Mars. Tim held the beautiful crystal out to show the captain. Amelia almost had a heart attack when she saw what it was.

"3T, where did he get that?"

"From a junk vendor, for like 5 UC. She said it was magic. Why?"

Amelia took it in her hand and watched as it stayed suspended in the air. She flicked the crystal, and as it spun, Amelia stated for it to show her Earth. A detailed image of Earth appeared. She flicked it again and stated Ultoria Prime. Ultoria Prime appeared. She kept doing this and every time, no matter the planet, it would appear.

"What is it?" 3T asked.

"This is an original World Atlas. I think it might be a True Atlas."

"A what?"

"They are the rarest tools in the galaxy. An atlas of every world it has ever seen. The ones people make now die after a few years. The True Atlas never dies. It can show you planets from 100,000 years ago or even older," Amelia said while flipping through planets.

"How is that possible?"

"They were made by the technology, maybe even the magic, of the god-aliens that the Ultorians wiped out so long ago," Amelia sighed as she replaced the crystal into Jason's bag before it transfixed her focus again.

"And we have one?"

"We apparently have a lot of things. I am proud of the two of you. Getting true treasures for almost no cost. The True Atlas might come in handy someday, but it is a little outdated with the technology we have now.""

Amelia plopped back down on the couch, tired and hurting. 3T, despite not always catching on, realized that Amelia was not angry that they had found the bracelets and the True Atlas, but rather, that she was not the person to find them.

"Amelia…"

"What?" Amelia replied as if she was annoyed.

3T paused while he considered what to say to make her feel better.

"So, did you want to show me that dress then?"

Amelia smiled as she looked up at Timolas.

"It is more like 10 dresses."

Chapter 12: Finally Sleeping

Everyone on the ship slept very well that night. Our unambitious hero, Jason, was the first to fall asleep that night, as has already been discussed. He slept very well that night. The previous couple of days were terrible. First, he was nearly killed by a Martian gang, and then he had to lay in one spot, unable to move, alone with his thoughts. Moreover, those thoughts had drained him more than he knew. Nearly every bit of emotional energy the boy had saved up by avoiding those thoughts now had to be used on the flood of negative ideas that swarmed him. It was miserable. He had never had a day where he had nothing that he had to do since his father left him.

So, when the teenaged boy finally got to the point where his body forced him to sleep, he ended up having a very restful, deep sleep. It was more restful than any sleep he had gotten in his foster home and more comforting than the pile of rags in that alley on Earth. It was a perfect night's sleep, except that he had the same dream that he had had two days prior.

A sword, his sword, stuck in a stone, waiting to be pulled. Jason was once again apprehensive of trying to pull the sword from its place of rest. He knew he was not worthy to wield it, let alone pull it from the rock. Jay was about to walk away this time, but he heard voices from behind him. He turned back to the stone to see Captain Amelia Hush and his best friend, Timolas Thomas Tymes. They were cheering him on!

"You can do it!" The dream Amelia yelled.

"We're here for you!" Spouted the dream 3T.

If his friends believed in him, even if he knew he would fail, Jason decided that he had to try. He strolled over to the sword. His hands gripped the handle. He lifted his leg to give him more leverage to pull! Finally, as he started to pull, Jay's eyes flickered open. It was already morning and late morning at that. He had no idea if he pulled the sword out or not. He assumed not.

The twins, Zeb and Zed, were the next to have fallen asleep. They took the rooms closest to the manual turrets, Zeb on the port and Zed on the Starboard. It was common that the twins would share a room, but they learned the value of privacy as they got older. Zeb never had the opportunity to have his own room as he always had to share with his brothers. Zed, being the only girl out of the twelve Tymes siblings, had been given her own when she turned ten. The twins, of course, fell asleep at the same time as each other, even when they were apart.

The twins slept better than they had in the entire last year. While they felt horrible for helping a gang mug and possibly kill their brother and his friends, they also felt safe. When they were first abandoned on Mars, they lived in an alley, much like 3T and Jay had on Earth. They were in constant fear that the gangs would come for them. They were right as the Red Dusters did come. The twins had to beg for their lives and had to prove they were absolutely broke.

The Red Dusters, having realized there was no monetary value in the twins, decided to offer them the chance to earn not being roughed up the same way Jason was later. Zeb and Zed had to accept. Anything was better than the street, right? The two of them slept in fear in the Red Dusters safe rooms. Their neighbors in the cots beside them had killed dozens of people over the years. The Red Dusters did not have many rules that kept members from killing each other, either. The hissing man had personally stabbed two people with the intent to kill in front of the twins on the first night there.

So, when the twins finally had beds of their own, on a ship dashing through the solar system, they felt like they were safe. No one was going to sneak up on them while they slept. No one was going to die. No harm would come to them. It was this safety that allowed the twins to sleep in all the way till mid-morning.

The last to sleep was the first to rise that morning. Amelia and Timolas only stayed up another hour after Jason was helped back to bed. The captain was honestly excited to get to show off her new clothes to 3T. She had never had a friend that took interest in clothes or her interests or her. Amelia barely knew how to act.

Timolas, having a huge crush on his captain, was more than willing to look at her clothes. Of course he thought she would just show him the clothes, but Amelia insisted on trying on each outfit and asking him his thoughts. 3T had very little experience with women, but he never would regret agreeing to Amelia's fashion shows.

It took Amelia roughly five minutes to change into the first outfit. The dark green dress brought out the best of her features including the natural blush in her cheeks. Timolas noticed immediately when she came back out from her quarters. He was speechless. Amelia, in that moment, was the third most beautiful sight that 3T would ever see. Amelia sat on the couch beside him after showing him how it flares out when she twirls. 3T was enraptured in the display, and Amelia had his full attention. The two friends sat and talked about the dress and the other outfits she had and all of the shops they visited on Mars and how 3T bought nearly a dozen belts. The two kept talking for the next hour with Amelia forgetting that she wanted to show off every dress she bought.

Eventually, Timolas had no choice but to doze off as he had not slept since the night before their short visit to Mars. Amelia did not blame him. Adjusting to living in space was difficult, Amelia knew. It had to be hard on a country boy like 3T, especially when your dream was to provide for your family. Space was just the bonus, the dream of every kid. Amelia smiled as she laid her friend down on the couch and covered him with a blanket.

The captain moved quietly to her quarters. She checked through the other door to see how Larriott was managing. The stalwart pilot was happily still guiding their ship through space.

Amelia shut the door to the pilotrest and moved to her bed. She decided to change out of her dress and put her red uniform back on. Then, as she had the previous two nights on the ship, she climbed underneath the bed and closed her eyes. Everyone was finally able to sleep.

Chapter 13: The Better Shots

Amelia was the first to wake up the next morning. She hardly ever slept more than four hours. The captain went through what she thought to be a normal routine for a captain. First, she checked on Larriott again. As he was when she went to sleep, the pilot was still focusing on flying the ship. Next, Amelia checked all of the ship's instruments to make sure the ship was not having any issues and then updated the navigation charts. Finally, she moved back through the pilotrest and through her own room to enter back into the living area.

"Mister Timolas, get up. Time for work."

Timolas rose up from the couch where he had fallen asleep the night before.

"Good morning to you, too."

"It is your turn to make breakfast, Mister Timolas."

"Can't it wait? It is barely 0500."

"No, I am hungry. Also, everyone else will probably want something as soon as they get up. No one, besides Larriott, ate well yesterday."

"Fine," 3T stated tiredly as he got up from the couch.

"Just fine, huh?" Amelia asked with authority.

"Yes, Captain. That better?"

"Yes, I will get the room cleaned while you cook. Your siblings are supposed to fix the table, if they can."

"Want me to wake them?" 3T asked before entering the kitchen.

"No, let them sleep. They are going to have a lot of work to do. Including getting familiar with the turrets."

"Fine."

Timolas should have finished making breakfast quicker than Amelia could clean the living area with how fast food orbs made cooking, but as soon as 3T entered the kitchen, Amelia considered cleaning the room a challenge. She used every skill she had learned from years of various martial arts classes and translated them to straightening up the room. If anyone saw her, they would say she was a tornado of red flames. Misplaced books, board games, and pillows were kicked, tossed, and punched right back into the places they belonged. The decorative rugs and displaced furniture were straightened in mere moments. By the time 3T entered with breakfast, which only took him a few minutes, Amelia was lounging on the couch with the room being perfectly fixed except for the broken table.

"How did…" 3T started.

"Practice," Amelia answered before he finished while also taking a plate of bacon and Mama Mack brand pancakes.

The two ate their breakfast while talking about their plans for the day. After Amelia said she planned on training, it was only natural for 3T to ask to join in. While 3T knew that a hand-to-hand fight would lead to him being absolutely destroyed, he thought he might have a chance with laser pistols. Amelia, who hated losing, decided to wager on the competition. They each got three shots with the little A-Class practice pistols on a small target that was far too thick to be damaged any more than leaving a small burn mark. Closest to the middle, a red dot painted on by the captain, from the furthest distance away won.

The first shot each took was from about 10 meters. Each shot was perfectly centered. They knew that they had to step back further to win. As they started to move to the next location to fire from, they both realized that they could not let the other step further back than themselves. So, the two teens each stood the full 20 meters of the room away. The second shots were the same as the first ones, dead center. There was only one solution. They set the target up at the longest unblocked part of the ship, the hallway into the living area which was over 30 meters.

3T fastened the makeshift target to the door to Amelia's room. They were to stand at the door to the engine room to ensure neither could take a step back. Amelia took aim, first.

PHEWF

The shot was less than a quarter inch from center. They measured to get an exact measurement before 3T got to shoot his shot. 3T stood in the exact same spot. He aimed. He fired.

PHEWF

It was just as far from the center as Amelia's. Even worse though, the twins had awoken and left their rooms, simultaneously, just in time to witness 3T's shot.

"Pathetic," started the twins in unison.

"What? No, that was dead center," 3T objected.

"Nope, half an inch off," Zeb teased.

"Might as well be a mile," Zed continued.

Sure enough, when Amelia and 3T measured the distance, it was exactly a half inch off, the same as the captain's shot.

"I guess it is a tie," Timolas sighed in relief that he would not have to go through with the competition's forfeit.

Amelia, annoyed at her failure to win, turned towards the twins, "Better than anything you two could do."

"Ah, but you are wrong, captain," Zeb replied.

"Very," Zed continued as she picked the little A-Class lasers up.

"The thing is," Zeb continued as he took a gun from his sister.

"We don't miss."

At those words, Zeb and Zed dashed to the end of the hall as 3T and Amelia moved out of the way. The twins insisted on doing a roll at the end. As they popped out of the rolls, while still facing away from the target, two blasts came flashing from the twins' guns. Bullseyes. The second blasts came as they spun around. Bullseyes. Blasts three and four were in very quick fashion. Bullseyes. Fives. Bullseyes. Sixes. Bullseyes. Sevens. Bullseyes. Each shot was trickier than the last.

Amelia was speechless. 3T could hardly believe how accurate and quick their blasts were.

"I guess we proved our points," Zeb stated.

"Best go fix the table now," Amelia interrupted before the twins had a chance to continue. "And where do you think you are going, Mister Timolas? We both lost, we both give up the forfeit."

"Wait, no!" 3T objected.

"Too bad. We agreed. Loser lets the winner shoot them with the non-lethal A-Class practice pistols. I figure the leg would be the best part to be hit. Though you might have numbness in it for an hour or two. We will do it at the same time."

"Alright, but take your uniform off! I know it makes you immune to weak lasers."

"Oh, of course. I would never try to cheat you."

Amelia reached to unzip her uniform right there in front of 3T.

"Oh, actually, I think the leg just rolls up," Amelia stated right before she actually unzipped, seemingly unaware of what she was about to do.

3T was still blushing when he and Amelia picked the pistols up from where the twins left them.

"Together, Mister Timolas."

"Wait, close your eyes!" 3T exclaimed.

"What? Why?" Amelia questioned back.

"You can dodge lasers if you see them coming!"

"If I close my eyes, you will just move!"

"No, I won't."

"I won't dodge then!"

"Look, if I move, you will just kick my butt. If you dodge, what can I do about it?"

"Fine. I'll close my eyes."

True to her word, Amelia closed her eyes. They pointed, counted down from three, and fired. They both missed. 3T, knowing Amelia trusted him, did move to avoid being shot. Amelia, not actually trusting 3T not to move, decided to dodge when she heard 3T's voice shift in the direction it was coming from. She waited, knowing the blast would come just as the countdown finished and moved just in time to dodge the laser. It was an awful argument the kids had after that. It of course ended with Amelia shooting 3T out of nowhere, and 3T shooting Amelia when she helped him up off the floor. The captain refused to fall over or show how much it hurt her, but she did walk with a slight limp for about two hours.

Chapter 14: Coming Together

The rest of the morning went well. Amelia showed the twins the controls for the turrets, who were naturals at blasting with any kind of lasers. Larriott even approved them being allowed to blast some small passing asteroids. The twins did not miss. It was when they finished getting acquainted with the turrets and Amelia rejoined Timolas in the living quarters that Jason finally entered from his room.

"Good morning, 3T, Captain."

"Good morning, Mister Jason," Amelia greeted her friend. "How are you feeling today?"

"Bad, but better," Jason replied as he sat to eat some of the breakfast left on the now fixed table. "I need something to do. I don't like laying around."

"Mister Larriott and Mister Azion said bed rest and no physical activities."

"What about the D-MES? It is not physical and would keep him occupied," suggested 3T.

"Fine," Amelia relented. "How do you feel about that, Mister Jason?"

Jay thought on the idea for a second then decided, "Alright, I will use the D-MES, but I want to do it in the workshop. Why are you limping, 3T?"

"I beat Amelia in a shooting contest. Don't change the subject," Replied 3T.

"You did?"

"No, he did not, but it sounds like we have a plan then," Amelia said. "You can study while we practice our swordplay."

"You are just going to kick my butt again," 3T protested.

"Yes, I will. We all need to practice in case we end up in a fight. I, also, need to work the numbness out of my leg from where you underhandedly shot me."

Jason was quite confused about why Amelia and 3T were shooting each other, but he did not ask about it as he finished his breakfast. The captain and Timolas helped Jay down to the workshop/training room, even though he insisted that he was fine. The only issue Jason had was that he had no idea what class to have the D-MES emit. While the courses on magic, though Jay was skeptical that magic was real, were very tempting, Jason chose to study robotics, as that would benefit the crew the most in his opinion, and he really wanted to get the broken one that they found in the crate repaired.

As Amelia was showing 3T some techniques that would be very handy while using his laser daggers, Jay started to set the D-MES to teach him the basics of building and repairing robots. There was a screen connected to the helmet that allowed the user to shift courses and displayed feedback upon a successful use of the D-MES.[39] Jason was hardly paying attention to Amelia knocking Timolas to the ground as he set the machine to 'ROBOTICS.' It only took a moment for Jay to place the head gear on his head and set the D-MES to play.

Within that moment, Jay was no longer in the workshop watching his friends practice. He was watching someone explain the basics of robotics. He watched as the man explained how the circuits in the robots were connected. He saw an explanation on the various hydraulic joints that he might encounter. There were examples of welding, and a very long tutorial on how to read and repair basic code one might encounter in human and basic Ultorian robots. He watched as examples were given. He watched for days as these ideas and applications were shown to him. Finally, the D-MES finished the course.

Jason was back in the workshop. Only a few hours had passed in the real world. Amelia was still practicing her techniques, but 3T was nowhere to be seen.

"How did you do, Jason?" Amelia asked.

Jay looked at the screen of the D-MES, "I did fine. I got 30%."

Amelia smiled, "That is really good. I got around that the first time I took an advanced education certification course."[40]

"You took an advanced education certification course?" Jason asked.

"Yes. I have a 100% Mastery-level understanding of Economics, Extraterrestrial Relations, and I have a 60% Basic-level understanding of human history."

Jay was surprised at the captain's education. "You are 15 and have that much education?"

"Yes, I believe you could have, too, in the same life situation. You said you passed the basic education certification at

11, the first year of eligibility to take it. I did not pass until I was 12. Timolas said he passed at 15, which is not far from the normal age of 16."

"I actually got a 64% basic understanding the first, and only, time I took the basic education bit."

Amelia, amazed, asked, "You only took the certification once? How is that possible?"

"I mean, a 64% is barely passing. I wasn't allowed to take it again as I was sent to work the next day."

Amelia, still shocked that anyone she knew could finish basic education on the first try as only 0.0001% of people are able to pull off that feat, wondered at how much potential that kid she found in an alley had.

"You should keep taking these courses, Jason. Understood?"

"Yes, Captain. Might as well anyway while we are traveling through space and I'm still sore."

The captain walked with Jason back upstairs. It was late in the day at that point. Amelia and Jay found that the twins had made dinner when they entered into the living quarters and had it placed on the table they fixed earlier that day. Amazingly, it was pizza. Amelia, who had never eaten pizza due to her strict father, had never tried any food so amazing. Jason, who had not had pizza since his father left, thought the food was absolutely perfect. The twins thought it was pretty good, too, but it had not been as long since they had eaten the food.

Larriott was very appreciative of the teens bringing him a plate. The pilot also wanted to inform them that he will manage to get outside the solar system in only two more days, but he needs to take a break in a few hours.

3T, curious, had to ask, "How do you stay awake for days at a time, anyway?"

Larriott, without looking away from the ship's path, started to explain, "Well, I am a cyborg. I have enough cybernetic implants that supplement my Circadian rhythm.[41] So, now I follow a 96 hour cycle instead of a 24 hour one."

"So, you only need to sleep every four days?" Jay asked.

"Yeah, but I still get all of the rest I need after about six or seven hours."

"That explains the creepy look," The twins mumbled together just loud enough for Larriott to make out.

"HEY! I'm not that creepy. Besides, I was made this way. Cloning technology was not that advanced when I was designed."[42]

"What!?" Jason, 3T, Zeb, and Zed blurted out together.

"I am going back to the living area," Amelia sighed. "I have heard this story."

The four other teens could not believe that Amelia was not interested in hearing the story, even if it was old news to her. She left to go back to the living area. She knew the Larriott loved telling stories, but she had little patience.

"Well, kids, I am a clone as I said," Larriott started to explain. "However, I am kind of a failed clone. I was the third attempt to clone Earth's greatest starship pilot, Lawrence E. Pritchett. The first clone, an attempt to copy the Ultorians' technology, decided to be called Larry. He ended up having no emotions and murdered 12 people. I believe he escaped to become a pilot on some pirate ship. The second clone, who took on the name Elliott because of a need to feel different, had too much emotion, but not enough physical strength to undergo cybernetic implants. He, well, isn't around anymore. So, they combined Larry's formula with Elliott's and created me, Larriott. I look… wrong, but they allowed me to live a full life as a normal person. I heard the clone after me was a complete success, but I have never met him."

"That explains a lot of the questions I had, but what about your implants?" 3T asked.

"Ah, I found a benefactor that decided to test out how I would do given a chance, but he ended up going a different way after he bought the implants."

"Who was the benefactor?"

"Antonio De Salina."

"That ass!?" The Tymes siblings yelled together.

"Yes, him. It is actually how I learned of this spaceship. I was at his house, leaving after being fired, and overheard his oldest child telling his friend, our captain, Amelia, about the ship. Amelia noticed I had heard and found how to contact me. She had a plan to escape her upper-class life, but needed a pilot. That brings us here."

"Well," Jason started to say. "That explains everything I think. I am glad that Amelia just happened to be there that day to get you two connected. Thank you for telling us everything, Mister Larriott."

"Yeah, thank you," 3T added, not catching the hint. "Let's go see what Amelia is doing."

The teens were very grateful that Larriott told them his odd backstory, but Jason took the story as confirmation about Amelia's goals. As the group rejoined the captain, they entered the living area to a surprise. Amelia had made popcorn and had brought all of the pillows and blankets, which were dozens, from her master suite into the living quarters.

"What's this?" The twins asked together.

"Well, this is the first night we are all healthy enough to be moving about. So, I was thinking," Amelia said while losing the confidence in her voice, "Maybe, we could have a movie night."

The twins looked at one another and 3T and Jay looked at each other. Amelia had never had a movie night with friends, and, despite how she wanted to be seen as a fearless captain, she also wanted to have friends, the thing she had lacked the most in her life.

"Heck, yeah!" The twins answered first.

"Let us shower," Zed continued.

"And get fresh uniforms first," Zeb finished.

"I love the idea of a movie night," 3T agreed.

"I've never had one," Jay mused. "We should get cleaned up, too. I still have Martian dirt in my hair."

They laughed as Jason knocked some dirt out of his hair.

Amelia was beyond happy when she said, "Alright, go get cleaned up. Miss Zed, feel free to use my shower before me. I also have spare pajamas if you would like them. You can all borrow some pajamas, but you boys might look silly."

"I think we will be fine," Timolas replied. "Zeb can borrow some casual clothes from me."

The boys rushed off to the showers while the ladies went to Amelia's quarters to use her personal bath. The boys did not take very long to get clean. Even Jason, who nearly always had to sit down in the shower, was in a rush as they were all excited for movie night. 3T was willing to do anything to spend more casual time with Amelia, Zeb was just a huge fan of movies, and Jay had never had a movie night with friends as he had never had any friends, either. The girls, while being equally excited, took more time. Amelia was surprised how long it took Zed to shower, but the twin, being two years older and much more experienced with similar social situations, explained that she needed to smell good at parties, even ones like that.

Amelia thought she understood and for the first time in years took a long, hot shower. The captain had since she was just a small child kept herself on a busy schedule. She never relaxed as she went from one martial arts class to the next and then studied with her D-MES and went with her father on business trips to learn how to be successful. This schedule made her prioritize taking very quick showers. She had also never had a female friend, sister, or even remembered her mother. So, she took the advice Zed gave her to heart.

It took the girls nearly a full hour to get ready. So, it should not have been surprising when the girls exited Amelia's chambers, both wearing adorable pajama sets, that they found the boys wearing elastic waist shorts, plain t-shirts, and holding practice swords in their hands.

"What do you think you are doing?" Amelia asked in an annoyed, authoritative tone as she walked in on the three boys sword fighting. "You know Jason is hurt!"

"I'm feeling fine, Captain," Jason interjected as he dodged a light swing from Zeb. "The stuff they injected me with already has me almost feeling almost back to normal, at least good enough to fight these scoundrels."

"Yes, but," Captain Amelia was impressed with the dodge, even if Zeb was going easy, but still was worried about Jay's health.

3T gave a signal to Zed to indicate that they had swords, too, while Amelia was engaged in talks with Jason. Zed smiled as she quietly lifted the sword that was left for her behind the captain's back. The twin swung.

Amelia, who had not been hit in a fair fight in over three years, correctly read the signal that 3T gave in her peripheral vision. As she spoke to Jay about how irresponsible it was to fight while hurt, even though she still had not had her own rib injury treated, ducked under Zed's blow.

As Amelia grabbed the practice sword that was left for her beside the door, she turned towards her crew and said, "Fine, we will fight."

"Rules," Jason started to say. "Zeb and 3T told me how you destroyed them in training yesterday. So, we each get five lives. Any hit takes away one. You get only one."

"You sure you don't want ten?" Amelia asked mockingly.

"Five is fair, for now. Besides that, free-for-all, winner chooses the movie," 3T added.

"Deal," The twins added in unison.

"On the count of three, we start," Jay stated plainly.

"Three," Amelia started.

"Two," Jason continued.

"One," 3T counted.

"Go!" Yelled the twins in unison.

The twins went immediately for Amelia. Meanwhile, 3T was stopped by Jason. Amelia quickly took two lives from Zeb and three from Zed. The twins decided to retreat, but ended up getting engaged by 3T and Jay who had each lost a life to each other. Each twin managed to take a life from Jason, but Zeb lost one to 3T. Amelia, seeing an opening, dashed into the fray. It was quick. She managed to take the twins down to their final lives and take two from 3T only a few moments after having joined the battle.

The three could not hold Amelia off as Jason tried to sneak up behind. Jay only barely dodged her strike. If he was not being cautious from still being a little sore, he would not have. When Amelia turned towards the twins and 3T, the youngest Tymes child did the unexpected. He struck, taking away both of Zeb's and Zed's final lives. They were annoyed, but admitted they would have done the same, if they thought about it, since it was just a game.

"Two lives versus one," 3T pointed out. "I can give up one to land a blow."

"Try it then," Amelia mocked.

True to his word, 3T tried it. All he had to do was let her hit him and return a blow at the same time. A strategy like that would have worked against anyone else on that ship. Amelia was not anyone else though. Even if 3T had not told her the plan, she assumed that was the end goal. Amelia struck faster than 3T realized she could. He had lost a life, and before he could land his blow, Amelia parried. A final blow from the captain finished Timolas off before he had any idea what happened.

"Good try," Amelia teased.

The captain turned towards Jason.

"Last two standing, Mister Jason."

"One life each, as well," Jay stated firmly.

"Show me what you have."

Jay engaged Amelia who transitioned into a more defensive stance. While she could easily dodge, she wanted to test Jason to see what he could do. She also did not want the boy to feel bad for losing as she thought he was hurting. Jay, who was feeling almost back to normal, went in and gave it everything he had. 3T whispered to the twins as his two friends fought. Jay put up a good show, but he was sloppy, untrained, and could never beat Amelia in a fair fight. Very few people in the galaxy could. So, when Amelia saw all she wanted from the boy, she delivered a soft strike to his arm.

"Amazing, Captain," 3T said as the fight was over.

"Very," Added the twins.

"Go on, take a bow," 3T prompted.

"Very well," Amelia accepted, proud of her victory.

The captain turned towards her friends and crew, the three Tymes siblings, and took a deep bow. As she raised up from her bow, she felt a soft tap on her shoulder. She turned to see what had tapped her, but only saw Jason, sword still in hand. The siblings burst into cheers!

"What?" Amelia asked in a confused tone.

"I lied. I had two lives left."

"But," Amelia started.

"It's true. I kept count. He only took one strike from each of us," 3T interrupted as he went to hug Jason.

Amelia, angry and proud at the same time, stated, "That was a good plan, Mister Jason."

"It wasn't mine. 3T told me what to do. Take a strike from you to lose one life to create an opening."

3T smiled and teased, "I didn't think you would catch on. I'm not known for my plans."

Amelia was furious at losing again, but she was so proud that her crew beat her and figured out how to do it together. She put away the swords and they all piled onto the couch and pillows and blankets. 3T suggested a space movie for Jason to pick. Amelia wanted a Kung Fu flick. The twins demanded a movie with fast cars. Jason picked the one where a kid ends up on the hunt for a pirate's lost treasure. They all agreed, it was the perfect movie.

Chapter 15: As a Crew

The teens all started to doze off that night while piled up together on the couch and the blankets on the floor. It was the twins who fell asleep first, both leaning on each other on the couch. They had remained very busy since arriving on the ship. 3T only managed to stay up later than the twins because he wanted to talk to Amelia more, but he did eventually fall asleep on the blankets on the floor next to Amelia's legs. The captain would have gone to her own room, but she did not want to accidentally wake her crew.

It was not very long after the second movie finished, an old American western, that Larriott idled the ship down to a slower, safer traveling speed so he could get some sleep, too. So, it was only Amelia and Jason who were still awake aboard the unnamed vessel.Amelia was surprised that Jay had yet to fall asleep. Jay felt the same about the captain.

"Do you normally stay up like this?" The captain asked.

"No, but it isn't uncommon. I have trouble sleeping most nights."

"I do, too. I have bad dreams, or I am just too busy to sleep."

"I hate that I dream, Amelia. The world inside my head isn't so bad, but I still dream of my dad, though."

"I'm sorry he left you, Jason. I know the feeling. My mother left me when I was a baby and died several months after."

"I'm sorry she left you. Though, you did leave your family, too."

"That is different. You would not understand the terrible things my family would do just to see a profit."

"I think I do understand. I did work in the De Salina Salt Mine."

Amelia was shocked at his choice of words, but before she had composed herself enough to decide if she should just ask Jay if he knew, a quiet beeping and a little yellow light started to flash.

"What's that, Captain?" Jay asked as he stood up from where he was sitting on the floor beside the sleeping 3T.

"It is a radar warning. It means something is moving towards the ship. Come on, let us go check it out," The captain suggested.

Amelia and Jason carefully got up, doing their best not to wake the Tymes siblings. They climbed up the hatch into the main deck, and Amelia went over to some screens and started to fiddle with some settings.

"So?" Jay asked as he approached Amelia.

"It looks like three small ships are approaching us. We must be going at a slower speed," Amelia explained as she watched a screen displaying three objects moving towards a larger one in the center of the screen.

"What do we do?"

Amelia moved over to another seat. That one had a transmitter, much like the one in the pilotrest. She messed with some dials until she found the incoming ship's local frequency.

Amelia cleared her throat and spoke into the machine, *"This is a yet to be named vessel. I am Captain Hush. State your business in approaching my ship."*

A moment passed before a reply came.

"This is Captain Hugo, leader of a small fighter squadron hired to protect trade routes between the Uranus and Neptune mining colonies. We picked up an unregistered flyer class vessel moving at an idle pace.[43] We decided to check it out. Permission to approach."

"Permission granted, but slow your pace of approach."

As Amelia finished her statement, she turned towards Jason with a nervous look on her face.

"Jason, wake the others. Send Timolas to the pilotrest with myself and Larriott. Send the twins to the turrets. You come back here and manage the radar and comms."

"What? Why?"

"The mining colonies of Neptune were shut down two years ago due to a lack of profits. There are no trade routes between those two planets anymore. These guys are not who they claim to be. Now go. This is an emergency."

Jason rushed down to the living quarters and immediately started yelling for everyone to wake up. The siblings rose tiredly, only having fallen asleep a couple of hours earlier. Before they could ask what was happening, Jay told them that they were about to be intercepted and explained where the captain wanted each of them to go. The twins and Timolas asked no questions since they were all terribly nervous about what being intercepted meant.

Jay returned to the main deck and sat at the radar station. He had little idea how to operate it, but he put on the headset hanging on the station anyway. He immediately heard Amelia's voice.

"Come in, this is the ship's on board comm system. Please report in when you have made it to your station."

Amelia was repeating that phrase, clearly hoping for a response.

"This is Zeb, at the port side turret."

"This is Zed, at the starboard side turret."

Before Jay could report he was on radar, Amelia came back on the comms.

"Good. Three ships are incoming. Intentions unknown. Hold fire until ordered otherwise. Mister Larriott, what is our status on going back to traveling speed?"

Larriott's voice started playing through the comm, "I will have us back to traveling at top speed for inner solar system speed in twenty minutes. Mister 3T has just joined me."

"Mister Timolas, report in," Amelia ordered.

"I just took the co-pilot chair. Larriott is already explaining the forward cannon controls and having me help prepare for rapid acceleration."

"Roger. What about the radar, Mister Jason?"

"I am still fidgeting with the dials," Jay answered as he played with the dials. "We have only a minute, according to the current screen, before they are almost on top of us."

"Good, keep Mister Zeb and Miss Zed updated on possible shots. I am about to call the fighters again."

Amelia changed the frequency of her comms in the pilotrest to communicate with the oncoming fighter squadron.

"This is Captain Hush. State your true intentions or we will treat you as oncoming enemy vessels."

There was a long silence before the leader of the squadron replied, *"Your ship matches descriptions of a ship stolen from our employer. We have been ordered to patrol the system to find the ship. If your ship is not the one we are after, we will move on our way. If that is our ship, we will incapacitate and impound it."*

"Feel free to check the ship, Captain Hugo."

Amelia turned her comm back to the on ship communications.

"Crew," The captain started. "Fire when ready. Take defensive action. Those ships are De Salina's goons. They will have our heads for stealing this ship if they win the fight."

Everyone on the ship was nervous. 3T had little training in the pilotrest and was worried about having to open fire. He had only shot one person before, and that was the other day on Mars. The twins had less apprehension on taking fire on people. They had been forced to fight in the Red Dusters, but they had only ever killed one man before, the hissing man. Jason was terrified he would mess something up. He was not in a position to attack, but it was important for him to read the radar, a machine he had never used before, and relay that knowledge to his friends. Amelia was ready to kill, but she needed to keep her crew's heads in the fight.

Larriott came back on the comms, "Feel free to switch the turrets and forward cannon to the non-lethal shock setting after you lower their shields and burn off their laser defenses."

The Tymes siblings were glad to hear that they had a non-lethal option. Amelia was worried that letting them live would just lead to more trouble when they reported back to their boss. She did not want to contradict her pilot, though, and she knew that it was the right thing to do.

"The three ships are splitting off in different directions," Jay spoke over the comms. "One is still coming straight from the back, left. One is splitting off to move towards the front of the ship. The other is trying to get on our right side upon approach."

Larriott piped in before anyone else could say anything, "Please refer to our left as port, our right as starboard, our front as the bow, and the back as stern. As if we were on a nautical ship."

"Yes, sir," Jay Replied. "They are right on us now. The one on the port side is moving forward."

"Boogie spotted," Zeb stated.

"Fire when ready," Amelia ordered.

"Gotcha."

Zeb fired as soon as he got the turret pointed at the ship flanking on the port side. He did not miss. The fight had begun. The V-Class laser turret eroded through the small fighter ship's shields. The fighter, now with no protection, dove under the unnamed flyer vessel. The fighter that was flanking towards the starboard side opened fire right after. The fighter's T-Class lasers crashed into the much larger ship's shield. The flyer had a stronger shield, and its much larger size made it able to sustain many more hits that the flyers could take.

The ship that was still coming up from behind started firing towards the back main thruster of the flyer. Luckily, Jay had found a setting on the radar that showed a 3-D model of the ship and the objects within 2,000 meters of it.

"Ship on starboard side. One moved from the port side to underneath us. Final ship quickly approaching from behind," Jason blurted to the crew over the comms. "Sorry, from the stern."

Larriott did not waste any time. The pilot quickly pulled the ship to the left, the port side. The flyer spun free from the three fighters, leaving them all on the starboard side. Zed also had an opening on one of the ships as the spin stopped. She took the shot, and it did the same damage as her twin's did to the first fighter.

The three fighters changed course to now intercept the flyer at the same time. They all opened fire, but only one blast hit. The ship's shield held firm, but did flicker a little. Larriott pulled back on the ship's controls to reduce their speed. Now two of the ships, the ones with downed shields, were in front of the unnamed ship. 3T quickly switched the forward cannon to the shock mode and fired. It was a beautiful shot. Both of the enemy ships ahead were now stunned and out of the fight. Larriott quickly twisted the ship around the downed fighters.

"One ship left on radar," Jay announced as they sped through space. "Directly under us."

"Roger," Amelia replied. "Get the twins a shot, Mister Larriott."

Larriott tried to flip the ship over and behind the fighter, but the smaller ship had too much of a mobility advantage. Larriott could not easily out maneuver the smaller ship. Jay read out the fighter's location as Larriott performed spins, dives, barrel-rolls, braking techniques, and any other idea to get a shot on the remaining fighter. The fighter was too quick, though. It dodged away from Zed's next blast, and Zeb thought it was moving too quickly when it had spun around to their port side. It seemed to be a stalemate. The fighter was more maneuverable, but Larriott was one of the best human pilot's in the galaxy or at least a clone of one.

The two ships kept flying and circling, trying to gain any kind of advantage. Finally, Larriott found a strategy that worked. The old clone started to spin the ship madly! The fighter had to increase its distance from the flyer to avoid being slapped by its spinning wings. Jason gave the twins and 3T the exact location of the fighter in relation to their own ship. Amelia swapped her comms to communicate with the fighter.

"Mister fighter, we hereby accept your surrender. Feel free to return to your base to get help for your squad mates."

The fighter, Captain Hugo, responded, *"Your ship can barely take any more hits. Your shields will fall. Surrender yourself."*

Amelia knew the message was a success. The fighter pilot had to split just enough attention away from engaging with the unnamed flyer to reply. Larriott got enough distance away by pulling down from the spin. He had just had enough space to force their ship to take a sharp turn towards the fighter. The fighter, knowing he could not let an approach at that angle, shifted to dive straight at the flyer. It was a game of chicken as the two ships quickly approached a head on collision. Captain Hugo knew he could shift out of the collision just in time, and that the forward cannon on the flyer could not down him in one shot, and the turrets would not be locked on in time to fire on him. He decided to take aim and finally blast away the unnamed vessel's shields.

Larriott took the hit, as he knew that the trap was already being sprung. The entire time the ships had been shifting towards and then speeding towards each other, Jason kept the Tymes siblings well informed with very accurate information of where the fighter was. So, the turrets were already locked on to the location the fighter would be in front of them. The twins, who were nearly perfect with their aim, and 3T, who was only a little worse than the twins, all fired together. Just like in the sword fight the night before, they took a hit to deliver a final blow.

The fighter turned into a ball of fire in a flash, but as quickly as it was aflame, the oxygen burned away, leaving only a charred, frozen chunk of wreckage.[44] It was over already. Larriott dodged around the remains of that final enemy vessel and zoomed their ship off into the distance. The crew all let out cheers as they had won a three on one space battle. Amelia was extremely proud, as the crew worked perfectly together. The twins were beyond excellent with any kind of blasters. 3T had managed to stay composed and followed all directions from Larriott to perfection. Larriott himself was a better pilot than even Amelia could have ever imagined, and Jason, that boy that lived in an alley, had managed to figure out the radar and all of its settings and even gave detailed coordinates on that final fighter's location. The captain doubted she could have done such a good job herself.

They won their first battle, and they did it as a crew.

Chapter 16: Blood in the Void

It was not long before Larriott had the ship back to an accelerating state. He informed the teens that he needed sleep, but it was not safe until that made it outside of the solar system and could transition the ship into a Solar Drive travel lane.

"Can you teach me to pilot early? Before we leave the system?" 3T asked, trying to be helpful.

"Hmm, yes, but only if you have a navigator while I am asleep for the first bit after I show you," Larriott responded.

"Wonderful," Amelia interrupted as she got up to leave the pilotrest. "I will show Mister Jason how to navigate using the radar, and he and I will help navigate you together."

"Great idea, Captain," Larriott responded. "It shouldn't be hard to pilot the ship. You'll mostly just steer. The buttons and switches come later."

"By the way, that was wonderful piloting back there, Mister Larriott, and very fine shooting, Mister Timolas," Amelia said, praisingly.

The pilot and soon-to-be co-pilot were both happy to receive praise on their performance. Amelia left the room to the main deck as the Larriott began to show 3T the controls on the ship. The captain entered to find that the twins had already climbed up to join Jason in the main deck. They were talking excitedly about the battle, and the twins were heaping praise onto Jay, who felt a bit uncomfortable as he felt he did not actually do much to help.

"Every shot was exactly where you described," Zeb praised.

"Indeed, and you were excellent at describing where that last bastard was," Zed continued.

"Language," Amelia playfully stated as she joined the group. "Miss Zed, Mister Zeb, feel free to go back to sleep. I have to teach Mister Jason how to navigate so we can give Mister Larriott a break."

"Sure, captain," The twins shrugged together as they jumped down the open hatch back down into the living area.

"So, Mister Jason, great job with the radar," Amelia praised. "You picked it up faster than I think I could have if I had to learn it the old fashioned way."

"Thanks, Captain," Jay said, but still felt unsure about the value he added to that fight.

"I am going to show you how to navigate," Amelia continued. "Simple really, you just have to inform the pilot of upcoming obstacles."

"Alright, sounds good," Jason replied while still being unsure.

Larriott made sure that 3T knew what every control in the pilotrest did. The teen was not the fastest learner, but he did have a talent for it. Larriott assured him that, for the most part, he would only have to dodge a few space rocks or move out of the path of a larger ship, if he was unlucky.[45] Of course, Larriott let the tired teen sleep a while after being shown everything, and the pilot showed 3T the controls again before going to take a much deserved rest himself.

Amelia and Jason studied the radar for a little while, but the captain was more than impressed with how quick the boy learned. Jay would easily surpass her at this skill, Amelia thought. Eventually, the two teens did drift off to their rooms to sleep before beginning the navigation process for 3T in a few hours time.

Amelia, who barely ever slept more than a few hours anyway, could barely rest as she laid on the floor under her bed. It was her fault those ships were after them. She was to blame for her crew almost being captured by the cruel Antonio De Salina. If it was not for Larriott's great piloting they would have been easily overwhelmed. If it was not for 3T, and his siblings that she reluctantly took onboard, they might have been the fireball hurtling through space. If it was not for Jay's quick mind, they would never have been able to get into the right position to win that fight. Amelia thought she had hardly done anything.

Jason had similar feelings. Amelia could have done what he did, most certainly better as well. Moreover, it was her plan. He would not have been able to shoot the shots that his best friend and his siblings made. He could not even imagine being able to pilot like Larriott. He felt like he needed to contribute to the crew more. He never thought that he would be good enough for them. He was wrong, of course, as most people who think like that are.

It was still early in the morning when 3T began to pilot the ship. Larriott stayed awake for a while to help guide the teen, but soon saw that Timolas had already figured the basics out. With Amelia and Jason helping spot upcoming objects, Larriott felt it was plenty safe enough to doze off for a few hours. Zeb and Zed made breakfast and brought it to the crew, but their younger brother was far too nervous flying a ship through space to eat.

Amelia and Jason only had a few bites to eat. So, the twins ended up devouring enough food for the entire crew themselves.

3T only had to maneuver around one small asteroid. Amelia and Jason spotted it with plenty of time for the would-be pilot to dodge it. Of course, only having ever flown it in a straight line, Timolas dodged in the clumsiest way possible. He managed to flip the ship over eight times before he managed to pull back on course. It was wonderful for a beginner.

Time seemed to fly by as it was not long before Larriott was back awake. The real pilot was very proud of his new protege. Larriott took back over piloting, but promised to let 3T practice all he wanted once they got past light-speed.[46]

Larriott, now back in control, made an announcement to the crew over the intercom system:

"Attention crew. We have made it roughly 5 AU into the Kuiper Belt.[47] We will be traveling at roughly 1 AU every two and a half hours. We will be moving into post-light-speed travel in 38 hours."

The crew were all nervous and excited at the news. None of them had ever been past Mars before they climbed on that ship, and now, they were about to fly out of their solar system. The Sun, now a bright star behind them, was moving further and further from these teenagers. Soon, it would be gone.

The crew all pitched in when it came to cleaning and cooking for the crew the next couple of days. Having gotten into a schedule of rotating who makes dinner and breakfast, the young crew all had plenty of time to do plenty of other things.

Jay, who Amelia was not convinced was fully healed, decided to focus on learning about robotics. He took the D-MES course a second time after Larriott took back over piloting, but only received a 54% understanding. Jason received a terrible headache from the second use, and 3T suggested he sleep it off. Which, he did.

As for 3T, he mainly played cards with his twins until dinner when Jay told him about the headache. 3T thought studying might be a good idea , himself, as he did not want to be caught off guard again. So, he used the D-MES to study piloting that evening, and received a 48% understanding thanks to the physical practice he had earlier that day. He was surprised Amelia was still awake and still training when his D-MES course finished after a few hours.

"So, how did the course go, Mister Timolas?"

"48%," 3T said as he stood up.

"Wonderful," Amelia stated before she had to ask, "Would you like to spar with me?"

3T, feeling very tired and still coming down from the false reality the D-MES created in his mind, politely said, "Sorry, Captain. I'm too tired. This thing drains the mind."

Amelia gave him a face and said, "Go to bed, then."

Not wanting to let the captain down, 3T made a suggestion, "How about tomorrow morning?"

Amelia was delighted at the suggestion, though disappointed she could not fight right then, agreed.

"That will work perfectly, Mister Timolas. I will wake you before breakfast for some training."

"Yes, Captain," 3T groaned, knowing he had already agreed and refusing to disappoint that lady.

Amelia continued on with her training as Timolas left. She liked that he seemed to listen to her, but she had yet to think of him as anything more than a friend. The captain was skilled in many things but love was not one of them. Maybe it was inherited from her father who had never truly loved anyone.

Amelia did not practice much longer as she was getting very tired, too. The captain decided to try and finish getting the registration device installed after Larriott took over piloting since he did not need a navigator. It was an annoying job, but after a few hours, the device started working. However, it apparently took hours to finish setting up and getting to the point where someone could register a name for the ship. So, Amelia went to eat dinner and then went to bed. It was while she was laying beneath her bed that she decided that she would name the ship with the help from her crew, but only once they left the solar system.

The next day was similar to the last. The teens got a few things done, here and there, but mainly, Jason and 3T took turns on the D-MES. Jason studied robotics again and only managed to improve to a 59% understanding. 3T was both being destroyed by Amelia in a sparring match and being shown more new tricks he could use with his laser daggers. He was rather bruised when he started his turn studying piloting on the D-MES and only improved to a 57%.

Amelia spent the next few hours after training trying to install the circuit that would allow them to pick up job requests from nearby star systems. She did not have much luck. Jay, on the other hand, decided to work on putting together the robot they found on the ship. Despite not completing the robotics course, he seemed to be doing really well. He managed to attach the arms to the already suspended torso and even managed to remove the outer casing of the body to be able to paint it later. He was in the middle of attaching one of the fancy hands from Azion's when 3T awoke from the D-MES.

"That is really good, Jay," 3T praised as he walked over to the dangling bot.

"Thanks," Jay smiled as he spoke. "I think attaching the other pieces won't be very hard."

"I'll help you paint it when it is time."

"Thanks, that won't be for a bit though. There is a lot I need to add. I also need to sort through the parts I got from Azion to see if any of them will suit this guy."

"I'm excited to see it when you finish."

"So," Jay decided to change topics, "How was your sparring session with Amelia? I forgot to ask earlier."

"She kicked my butt."

"No, I mean, did you make a move?"

3T blushed and said, "It isn't that easy. She is a badass, aristocratic starship captain. I don't think 'making a move' would work. She'd kill me."

Jay sighed when he replied, "You should tell her how you feel."

"Maybe. Anyway, want me to show you some moves before dinner?"

"Why not?"

The two boys practiced fighting for a bit, but knew that they could not be caught by Amelia as she would demand to take part. It was not long before the crew gathered for dinner, again. It was a joyous night as, when they woke the next morning, they would be leaving their solar system. The teens joked and laughed, and all were having a wonderful time at the table. It was a wonderful meal. Soon, they had found themselves talking into the night. The twins were telling stories of the gangs on Mars, 3T was telling the story of trying to sneak on a ship dressed as a Victorian-age woman, Jay told the story about he met 3T, and Amelia described how she won a martial arts tournament at the age of six that was meant for kids that were their ages now.

Jason looked at the clock and noticed something terrible while the twins were describing stealing a rare Martian fish. 3T and Amelia both noticed the face that Jay made when he saw what day it was. They hushed the twins.

"What's wrong, Jason?" Amelia asked.

"It's nothing," Jay lied, badly.

"No, tell us," 3T demanded.

"Yeah," Yelled the twins who had no idea what was going on.

"Well," Jay started. "Today is May 7th."

"And?" Everyone else asked together.

"It is my birthday tomorrow."

"What? Tomorrow?" Amelia asked.

"You never told me when it was," 3T stated.

"Congrats," The twins shouted.

Jason hung his head.

"No, he hates his birthday," 3T said, frustrated at the twins.

The twins looked at each other confused at why anyone would hate their birthday.

"He was put to work in a salt mine on his 11th birthday," Amelia started to explain, remembering their talks.

"And his father abandoned him on his 8th," 3T continued.

"And my mother died on the day I was born," Jay finished.

The room went quiet. The twins looked down. They were even more disappointed in themselves that they mugged that poor kid. Eventually, Jason stood up.

"I think I am going to go to bed."

Before anyone could say anything, Jason had left the room. The remaining crew talked amongst themselves. Jay hardly slept that night. He dreaded his birthday, and this year, he had something that could be taken from him.

He had only been asleep a few hours when a knock was at his door. Jason lifted his head up, but before he could say anything, Amelia burst into the room.

"Crew meeting. Meet on the main deck."

As quickly as she appeared, she was gone. Jason wondered what was going on, but he got dressed and went to go to the main deck. He climbed up to find everyone, besides Larriott, waiting on him already.

"What is going on?" Jay asked.

"We are about to jump to beyond light-speed," 3T stated.

"I wanted us to be here together when we did," Amelia stated.

"Alright, but…"

Before Jason could finish, Larriott came on the loudspeakers

"Crew, we are 30 seconds from departure from the Sol System. Current destination, Relictis System.[48] Destination subject to change."

Before Jay could say anything, the whole crew started the countdown.

"10, 9, 8…"

They are really excited about this, Jay thought.

"7, 6, 5…"

Jason started counting along at six.

"4, 3, 2…"

It was unbelievable. Jay went from an alley rat to a space adventurer in less than a week.

"1!"

The ship zipped off, as if it blipped out of existence. Jason was expecting cheers from his friends as they took off, but instead they horrified him. All four of the other teens pulled sharp pieces of metal from their pockets. In an instant they all used the sharp metal to cut open their palms. Jason was very confused and horrified as he had no idea what was going on.

"Jason," Amelia started to speak. "We have decided. Today, your birthday, we would all like to become your brothers and sisters."

"What?" Jay asked, still confused.

"Blood brothers," 3T explained. "We shake bloody hands to mix our blood and after we will be family."

"Family?"

"Damn straight," The twins exclaimed.

Before Jay could say anything, Larriott entered through the door, one hand already bleeding and holding up a birthday cake in the other.

"I want to be a blood great uncle. No offense, but you are all still a little young to be my siblings."

The crew all smiled. Jason looked at Timolas who had his head hanging low and approached him.

3T was surprised and said, "We don't have to do this."

Amelia, worried about how Jay held his head, started, "Yes, you don't have…"

Before Amelia could finish Jason snatched the metal shard from 3T. He looked up at the crew who were all now silent. With the same motion they performed, Jay sliced open his hand. Tears were already pouring from his eyes before he ever cut himself. This was an amazing gift to the boy. Never in a million years would he have thought he would have friends that would make a promise in blood to be his family.

"As your blood brother… and nephew, I swear I will always be there for you," Jason stated as he cried and held his hand out to Timolas.

Timolas and Jason shook their bloody hands together. Next the twins shook with Amelia and Larriott and then swapped to the other after. Jason shook Larriott's hand while the twins shook each others' hands, despite already being related by blood. Amelia shook Larriott's hand next as 3T turned away from her, as if refusing to shake her hand, to shake hands with his biological brother and sister. Amelia was pissed, but she let it go as she and Jason stepped up to each other.

"Jason," Amelia started. "I swear I will do everything in my power to ensure you are never left alone again. It is my duty as your captain and your new big sister."

Jason was bawling as the two shook hands. It was done. Finally, Jason had a family to call his own.

Epilogue

That is the start of the story of how an orphaned boy, Jason Calloway, who knew nothing of life except for its worst parts, found a family to call his own. He had to go through many struggles to get to the point where he is now, but he kept going. He made choices that led to the first steps of fixing himself.

By doing the right thing by offering his home, even if it was just an alley, and his bread to a stranger that seemed to be worse off than himself, he found himself a best friend, Timolas Thomas Tymes. He made friends with an aspiring space ship captain, Amelia Hush, by deciding to run back inside a building that he knew would be swarming with horribly armed guards, just to give his friends a chance to escape. In running back to help, Jason got to know an extraordinary pilot, Larriott the 'failed' clone. By making sure he did not let his captain down, he ran into a gang of ruffians. Two of which, Zeb and Zed, would never have been saved from a life of crime if he had not.

It was through those choices and those actions that Jason Calloway started the process to heal. He, after many years of despair, finally made a choice to keep going. It is still a long way to go as it is with everyone of us who deals with depression and anxiety and grief. Jason can learn to want to live again as anyone facing hardship can. He has a fight ahead, though, to feel worthy to draw his sword from the stone. However, he took the steps to get help. He is not alone. Neither are you.

Somedays, it will seem unbearable. Somedays, you will feel like you have no more fight to give. Somedays, you will feel like you are at your end. It will get better, though. There are people here to help you, but you have to make that choice to keep going, to keep fighting, to keep being you.

I said that at the start of this book that Jason was not special. My dear reader, I lied to you. Everyone is special and everyone has the ability to make a difference. Jason, he is us. So is Amelia, who feels undeserving to sleep in a bed or sit in her captain's chair due to sins she did not commit. So is Timolas, who gave up being with his family for the chance to find a way to provide for them elsewhere. So is Larriott, a man who never gave up on his dreams, despite being told he was a failure over and over again. So are Zeb and Zed, who had to resort to betraying their beliefs just to survive. No one is perfect and everyone has their own problems, but we can help each other through them, together, the same way the crew of that still unnamed space vessel will help each other.

The stories of these would-be space adventurers goes on. They will face off against robots and ghost assassins and scorned lovers. They will meet gods and immortal trees and rulers of empires. They will build new bonds and grow their family and grow as individuals. There will be heroes and villains in their paths, and they will be challenges that they would have never been able to imagine. They will find their places in the universe.

It is an unbelievable story, I know, but they will do it together.

Endnotes

1. There are many different versions of our planet. The basic theory is that there are an infinite amount of universes, and any possible action, possibility, or outcome has happened in at least one of them. The issue is, we only know the universe we are in based on the past. Many futures, even the ridiculous, are still possible in our universe and timeline.

2. Neolandia was a rather new city. By the time Earthlings had started trading amongst aliens, they had built up most of their old cities far too much to be able to fit decent space ports into them. So, they made new cities just for space travel. The city had already seen many changes. From a seemingly wonderful utopian city, to a horrific dystopia where homelessness ran rampant and then back to a normal city, except this time most people stayed on floating walkways, high above the ground level of the city.

3. He had, indeed, been out in the rain.

4. UC's are slang for Ultorian Credits, the most widely used currency in the Milkyway Galaxy.

5. New Mars was another new city. After the sea levels rose to overtake most of Florida, people were always looking for new ways to reclaim that land. That is when they pulled a chunk of Earth into the sky and built a city upon it.

6. Mama Mack is the galaxy's most famous baker. She also owns one of the largest food distribution companies in the Ultorian Empire.

7. Laser weapons are classed on Earth and the Ultorian Empire by letters. An A-Class weapon would be small enough to fit in your palm and would not kill, just sting a little bit. A Z-Class weapon, would shoot a continuous beam of energy and would vaporize diamonds and steel with ease. An N-Class weapon shoots non-continuous beams strong enough to kill, but not vaporize.

8. Just like laser guns, knives and swords can have the same classifications. An E-Class knife would be too short for much

outside of cutting open boxes or, with some work, canned food.
Though, it would leave a decent cut if stabbed straight on with one.

9. The Moon had been terraformed only a few years before
Mars, as a test of concept. However, things went overboard with
that space rock and it became a jungle that the Earth had not seen
since before Humanity existed. Of course, the same humans that
cut down Earth's jungles and grew a new one on their largest
satellite decided to turn it into a vacation get-away instead of
preserving nature with it.

10. Ultorian space encompasses hundreds of star systems.
The Ultorian Empire recognizes that it has 228 planets that contain
life and 88 species of intelligent life qualifying as citizens. It also
has 14 Protectorate planets that could join the Empire.

11. The conversion of 10,000 Earth credits would be
roughly 9.3 Ultorian Credits.

12. Water Crystals were first adapted from Ultorian
technology a few decades prior. The atoms of the water molecules

are all pushed together tight enough so that an entire lake, millions of gallons, could fit inside a crystal the size of a car.

13. Food Orbs were invented shortly after Water Crystals. They were mainly a human invention to help transport salt exports, but they quickly adapted to be very versatile. *Mama Mack's* is said to have perfected their use in the last thirty years. The orbs either need to heat up to 500 degrees or water, depending on the contents, to grow back into the food stored within.

14. He was madly in love.

15. "Go Find Peace."

16. Only two Earth companies make laser knives and blades, and only a dozen do in the whole galaxy. The katana, twin daggers, and pocket knife (and most blades in general) are Zommartom brand. The Attorium brand is far more beautiful and proved to be the best craftsmanship of any blade brand in the galaxy.

17. Exclon is a polyester-like material. It was invented by the warlike race of Folmosclonistarians before they realized they were far too small to conquer anything and became merchants.

18. Translator chips were a joint invention made by the Olnarians, not the tree people from Olnar II but the beetle-like race from Olnar I, and Ultorians. They were some of the first space farers to find each other in the void and made an organic insert to communicate with each other. Each species must adapt the insert for their own species, however.

19. Solar Drives are the devices that allow ships to travel faster than light. Instead of merely making the ship move fast, the drive allows the ship to form a tunnel into a different dimension to shorten the total distance between stars. There are also Galactic Drives that do almost the same but instead make a dimension that shortens a trip that would take a Solar Drive weeks to only days. Finally, there is a single Universal Drive which would make travel between galaxies feasible.

20. New Pacifica is one of the colonies that Earth had founded in the last few decades. The planet is almost all fresh water, but has thousands of islands which are all perfect for human habitation. It was only recently that humans discovered another intelligent species under the waves: the Subharans. They are rather clever, but the species has no desire to move past their own oceans.

21. Humans have invented very few technologies that other species had not already invented. Of these, the space bike is the greatest. Humans made bikes, more like jet skies, that could get almost all the way to the Moon. They use shielding technologies to protect the user and provide a pocket of air to breath.

22. Deimos and Phobos were, indeed, mostly forgotten by humans. The resources they found there were found elsewhere in greater amounts. This has made the moons a great place for pirates to hide within the Earth's solar system.

23. The radios found on most spacecraft, rather they be human or alien, are a collaboration invention between many

different species. In general, each time a new species finds its way into the galactic travel business, that species ends up improving the existing radio and transponder system. Humans contributed by adding the system to change frequencies to alleviate background noise.

24. Direct to Mind Education System. These devices were helmets that emitted educational courses straight into the brains of people. They speed up the time it takes to educate people, but it is still up to the individual to put in the time to learn the materials transmitted.

25. Human Earth Time

26. Void Bags were a collaboration between the Folmosclonistarians merchants and Z'lottes pirates. The Z'lottes, a slimy, fish-like people, figured out a way to make small space distortions, but needed Exclon to contain and sustain them.

27. The Folmosclonistarians were a little larger than an average sized beaver. They reminded humans of monkeys mixed with mushrooms. They inhabited most markets in those days.

28. It was getting more and more common for people to buy robots to run their businesses. Robots were only able to be so intelligent, as making them operated by fully functioning AI was highly illegal, but would also lead to having to pay them as the Ultorian Empire acknowledged those robots as 'sentient peoples' and did enforce a minimum amount of labor laws in its systems and its allies' systems.

29. Shop Keeping Assistant

30. The Red Dusters were a small gang in Blackfire. They were well-known, but there were much more horrible gangs in the town. It was a policy by the locals to ignore most gang activity, as it always led to trouble for any one involved.

31. Amelia was never going to let someone as horrible as to throw their friends into their deaths get away.

32. Amelia had rearranged the workroom in the bottom of the ship, instead of sleeping the previous night. So, half of it was a workshop and the other half was a training dojo.

33. Many smuggling ships came to Blackfire. It was the best black market town in the human controlled systems of the galaxy. *The Bad Break* was an infamous smuggling ship. It had never once made it to its destination in all of its 347 trips through space with all of its crew and cargo intact.

34. In honesty, 3T had spent most of the previous night running through how this conversation would go. He knew before he started asking questions to his siblings that he was going to fight them.

35. It was not hard for humans to make their transmissions for television and other forms of electronic communication go over the speed of light, especially after they managed to get spaceships to do so. However, it is common to pick up broadcasts from years before.

36. Yes, the people in the time of flying ships into space still played Rock Paper Scissors. The Ultorians actually took to it really well as they had actually made paper that could give diamonds paper cuts.

37. It was increasingly common for spaceship pilots to use a set of attachable arms so they could fly with four hands. The Ultorians had originally come up with the idea of mind controlled extra arms, but humans were one of the few species of aliens that could actually use them, but only after a very expensive telecommunication implant.

38. Tele-communication devices give people a pseudo-telepathy that allows communication across vast distances using one's mind. They were another Ultorian invention, but they used the magic they used from the ancient god-like race of aliens to create them so only a few alien species know how to make them.

39. The screens on the D-MES's can display information on the courses it teaches. Such as, the knowledge and skills it can

emit. It also displays how much mastery on the subject someone has. A 60%, a basic understanding, usually takes dozens of uses. For the basic education and advanced education courses, it takes a few years of use for the average person.

40. The D-MES has several different types of courses. The courses the crew are taking are just courses to teach skills. Official Advanced Certification courses would be the equivalent of a Bachelor's Degree. Basic Education at 60% would be the equivalent to finishing high school.

41. The Circadian rhythm is the natural cycle a human's body goes through that regulates changes in the body including when people get tired and need to sleep.

42. Clones on Earth were very rare. Only a few have ever been designed, but the Ultorians have developed so many that nearly a third of all Ultorians are clones or descendants of clones.

43. An idle pace in a solar system is roughly 54,000 MPH, at least for human ships.

44. Generally, there is no fire in space due to a lack of anything that can fuel the fire. However, when a ship is destroyed, all of the oxygen on board can combust.

45. While our current solar system has the asteroid belt between Mars and Jupiter, it also has the Kuiper Belt beyond Neptune. While there are many objects in the Kuiper Belt in our time, there are many more in the time of this story. Mainly because, while it is a mystery to most humans, Pluto and Charron were blown to bits at some point after they started to leave the Sol System.

46. The ship would not be going faster than light, but it would be traveling faster than it. The Solar Drive forced the ship into a different dimension before it hit light speed that made traveling a few feet into traveling a few miles..

47. Astronomical Unit is the average distance from the Earth to our sun or 92.955,807.3 Miles.

48. The Relictis System is home to New Pacifica, the Human colony.

Printed in Great Britain
by Amazon

86596030R00164